Ann's Story
1747

More stories in the

YOUNG AMERICANS

Colonial Williamsburg

SERIES BY JOAN LOWERY NIXON

CAESAR'S STORY: 1759
NANCY'S STORY: 1765
WILL'S STORY: 1771
MARIA'S STORY: 1773
JOHN'S STORY: 1775

Date Due

JUN - 1 2010		MAR 11 2011	

BRODART, CO.   Cat. No. 23-233   Printed in U.S.A.

A LETTER FROM

Colonial Williamsburg

The Colonial Williamsburg Foundation
Williamsburg, Virginia

Ann McKenzie was a real girl who lived in Williamsburg, Virginia, in the 1740s. Her father was an apothecary (a kind of druggist-doctor), and Williamsburg was the capital of the Virginia colony. Later, in the 1760s and 1770s, people in Williamsburg helped lead the thirteen colonies to independence.

Today, Ann's house and her father's apothecary shop are part of Colonial Williamsburg, a living history museum. Colonial Williamsburg's Historic Area has been restored to look the way it did at the time of the American Revolution. People in costume tell the story of Virginia's contribution to American independence and show guests how Williamsburg residents lived during the colonial era.

In Colonial Williamsburg's Historic Area, you can see where Ann lived and shop in the McKenzie Shop.

You can visit the James Geddy House and Benjamin Powell House to learn about the everyday life of families like the McKenzies, and maybe even do a few chores. You can find out about colonial medicine at the Pasteur & Galt Apothecary Shop.

The Colonial Williamsburg Foundation is proud to have worked with Joan Lowery Nixon on the Young Americans series. Staff members met with Mrs. Nixon and identified sources for her research. Colonial Williamsburg employees read each book to make sure it was as accurate as possible, from the way the characters speak to what they eat to the clothes they wear. Mrs. Nixon's note at the end of the book tells exactly what we know about Ann, her family, and her friends.

Another way to learn more about the life of Ann McKenzie and her family and friends is to experience Williamsburg for yourself. A visit to Colonial Williamsburg is a journey to the past—we invite you to join us on that journey and bring history to life.

Rex M. Ellis

Rex M. Ellis
Vice President—Historic Area
The Colonial Williamsburg Foundation

YOUNG AMERICANS

Colonial Williamsburg

Ann's Story

1747

JOAN LOWERY NIXON

The Colonial Williamsburg Foundation
Williamsburg, Virginia

Published by
The Colonial Williamsburg Foundation
PO Box 1776
Williamsburg, VA 21387-1776
www.colonialwilliamsburg.org

Colonial Williamsburg is a registered trade name of The Colonial Williamsburg
Foundation, a not-for-profit educational institution.

16 15 14 13 12 11 10 09 08   4 5 6 7 8

Library of Congress Cataloging-in-Publication Data

Nixon, Joan Lowery.
   Ann's story, 1747 / Joan Lowery Nixon.
        p. cm. — (Young Americans)
   "Colonial Williamsburg."
   Summary: Ann, a young girl in eighteenth-century Williamsburg, wants to
become a doctor like her father, but she is not allowed even to study Latin or
mathematics.
   ISBN 0-87935-198-5
 1. Williamsburg (Va.)—History—Colonial period, ca. 1600–1775—Juvenile
fiction.   [1. Williamsburg (Va.)—History—Colonial period, ca. 1600–1775—
Fiction.   2. Sex role—Fiction.]   I. Title.
   PZ7.N65Ao 2004
   [Fic]—dc22

                                                            2004050200
ISBN-13: 978-0-87935-198-4

Printed in the United States of America

Book design by Patrice Sheridan

Contents

Prologue

Lori Smith let out a yelp as Keisha Martin grabbed her arm, nearly pulling her off balance.

"C'mon!" Keisha said. "There's the market. Mrs. Hafferty told us we could look around Colonial Williamsburg until the other classes get here. We're early, so we've got plenty of time to buy caps."

Lori spotted a middle-aged woman setting up a booth. She was dressed in an eighteenth-century-style flowered print dress with an ankle-length skirt and wore a white, ruffled cap tied with a blue ribbon.

"Hurry up." Keisha gave another tug. "Here come Chip and Stewart. I bet they're going to want to buy cocked hats. Let's get there before they do."

The woman looked up and smiled as the two girls raced to her stall. "Good day to you, dearies," she said.

1

"I'm Mrs. Molly Otts, and I'm heartily pleased to welcome you to Colonial Williamsburg."

"Hi, Mrs. Otts," Lori said. "I'm Lori, and this is Keisha. We're here on a school field trip."

Chip and Stewart raced up. Chip crowded close, but Lori elbowed him aside. "Our teacher, Mrs. Hafferty, told us we'd be meeting interpreters throughout Colonial Williamsburg. They dress in eighteenth-century clothes and pretend to be actual colonists. Are you one of the interpreters?" she asked.

Molly Otts's eyes twinkled. "As you can see, I'm one of the vendors, come to market to sell my goods."

"I wonder what this market was like in the seventeen hundreds," Keisha said.

"I well recollect how each morning, as day first broke, vendors would begin unloading their vegetables and fruit, eggs, bread, meat, and fresh milk," Mrs. Otts explained. "With sheep bleating, cattle bawling, cart wheels creaking, dogs barking, and children running around underfoot and shouting, Market Square were a right noisy place. Not a fine way for a town to wake up! Don't you agree?"

Lori smiled. "I think it was Benjamin Franklin who wrote, 'Early to bed, early to rise, makes a—'"

Grinning, Chip interrupted. "Lori might be healthy and wealthy, but nothing's going to make her wise."

Lori ignored him and, turning toward Mrs. Otts, said, "Please tell us more about the market."

"Very well," Mrs. Otts said. "I've just told you how busy it was. Well, while all this hubbub was taking place, the farmers would quickly set up their stalls. No matter the weather—sun, rain, or snow—housewives, with their daughters and kitchen slaves, would soon arrive to fill their baskets with the food and provisions they'd need for that day."

Mrs. Otts looked up and studied the sky. "We can be thankful 'tis a fine day today, with no cloud in the sky and no look of rain," she said. "There'll soon be plenty of people out to shop, and I'm sure that the pocket I wear under my petticoat will be heavy with coins by nightfall. Over the years I've displayed my goods on many a market day, and I've never gone home disappointed."

"How many years?" Stewart asked.

"Ah, that would be telling," Mrs. Otts said. She beckoned to them, adding, "Pray step closer, and let me show you the goods I have for sale. Here are splendid cocked hats for young gentlemen and soft cotton and linen caps for young ladies. See—here's one trimmed with the brightest of blue ribbon. Every miss and every matron once wore caps such as these, even under their hats."

Lori immediately chose a soft white cotton cap with a blue ribbon. As she handed Mrs. Otts the money, Lori said, "It will be fun to wear this while I'm in Williamsburg, but I wouldn't like to wear it every day."

Mrs. Otts smiled. "You remind me of a rebellious young nine-year-old miss who couldn't abide wearing caps. Ann McKenzie was her name, and at times she found it difficult to obey the rules set up for proper young ladies to follow. Ann, with her high-spirited Scottish blood, had a difficult time behaving in a way befitting the daughter of a respected doctor and apothecary."

"My father's a doctor, too," Lori said.

Chip laughed. "And Lori doesn't always obey rules. Last week in math she—"

"Be quiet, Chip," Keisha said loyally. "Let Mrs. Otts talk about Ann."

"Ann's father was Dr. Kenneth McKenzie, who practiced medicine and who also owned the McKenzie Apothecary. You'll find it across Palace Green, next to the Robert Carter House. A good, kind doctor he was, a mite indulgent to young Ann, but—"

"What did Ann do that was rebellious?" Stewart interrupted.

"Oh, please don't get the wrong notion," Mrs. Otts said. "Ann was a dear girl in many ways and bright as a dozen lit candles in a looking glass. There were times

4

when she honestly tried to behave like a proper young miss. It's just that Ann's heart got set on something that everyone—even her beloved father—told her that she couldn't do. Would she listen? No, but . . .

"Wait. I'm getting ahead of myself." Mrs. Otts gestured toward a wooden bench. "Let's make ourselves comfortable, and I'll tell you Ann's story. I'll begin with the early-morning hours of Thursday, January 30, 1746/47—a terrible day when the Capitol building caught on fire."

Chapter One

Ann McKenzie was sleeping peacefully. She dreamed she was Dr. Ann McKenzie, sitting at the bedside of a sick child. But suddenly the child jumped out of bed, bright-eyed and well, and began shouting—shouting her name.

"Ann! Ann, wake up!"

Ann sat up so quickly she lost her balance and tumbled out of her high post bed.

"Ann! Wake up! Hurry!"

Fully awake now, Ann recognized the voice of her friend John Geddy. He had called from below the window of her bedchamber.

Ann scrambled to the window, threw open the sash, and leaned out. The dark night sky was just beginning to fade into gray, and the cold air made her shiver. The trees were freshly dusted with a heavy powder of snow.

Ten-year-old John, with his dark hair and eyes, gazed up at Ann from under a tree. "There you are," he said impatiently.

In delight, Ann laughed aloud. "Look, John! It snowed during the night!"

"Never mind the snow," John shouted. "Get dressed! Hurry! The Capitol's burning!"

"The Capitol?" For a moment Ann could only stare in amazement.

"Don't stand there goggling like a stupid fish," John scolded. "Hurry down, or I won't wait for you."

Ann pulled shut the window sash, reached for her chamberstick, and lit the candle in it. All the while she mumbled to herself, "Stupid fish, is it? Ha! *You're* the stupid fish! Don't think I'm obliged to do what you tell me to do because you're almost a year older than I! Don't you dare go to the fire without me, John!"

Ann groaned as she looked at her clothes, which had been laid out for her on the chair. She saw the stays that she would put on over the linen shift she had worn to bed. Her mother would lace the stays tightly. Next to them were white stockings, an under-petticoat, a flat pocket with a slit in it that she would tie around her waist, a quilted petticoat to wear over that, and a neatly folded gown made of a practical dark blue linen. On top of the gown rested a folded, bibbed apron and a white cap.

Dressing will take forever! Ann thought. *Stupid fish John will grow impatient and run to see the fire without me.* She also realized that if she asked her mother's help in fastening the stays, her mother would be more than likely to order her not to leave the house. She'd say that fires were dangerous, that children belonged in the safety of their homes, and that no proper young lady would willingly mingle with the noisy crowds that had come to gawk.

Ann didn't think twice about what to do. She pulled her woolen cloak from the chest, wrapped it over her shift, pulled the hood over her tangled red curls, and slipped her bare feet into her shoes. Then she picked up the chamberstick and stepped into the still darkened passage.

She paused by her parents' bedchamber, listening to the contented noises that young William—not yet two years old—was making as he nursed.

As Ann reached the foot of the stairs, she blew out the candle and placed the chamberstick on a nearby table. From here, even in the dim predawn light, she'd be able to find her way.

In the room used for dining, Ann could hear Myrtilla, the family's slave for as long as Ann could remember. From the thumps and scrapes she realized that Myrtilla—strong and capable—was setting up the table and chairs for breakfast.

"Get more wood for the fire, and fill the pot with water," Myrtilla said. Ann knew she was speaking to her twelve-year-old son, Silver.

The pot? Oh, no! It's washday! Ann realized. On washday housewives, children, and slaves rose early and were expected to help with this chore, which lasted for hours. *I'll only be a few minutes,* Ann promised herself. *I'll be home even before the water's hot.*

Quickly and silently Ann slipped through the back door, raced around the corner of the house, and ran to where John stood, scowling.

"What took you so long?" he asked.

"Would you have me run outside in my shift?" Ann retorted. Knowing that her shift was exactly what she wore under her cloak made her stifle a giggle.

John shrugged. "Girls!" he said with disgust. "We'll have to hurry, or the fire will be out before we get there." He turned and ran toward Duke of Gloucester Street.

Girls, indeed! Ann raced after John, determined to prove she could run just as fast as he, if not faster. As they reached Duke of Gloucester, she could see, near the end of the street, clouds of dark smoke and flashes of flame that shot toward the sky.

Others were running toward the blaze. Some of them shouted. A woman plopped down on the steps of Shields Tavern and burst into tears.

Puzzled, Ann stopped and turned toward her. "Do you need help?" she asked.

The woman shook her head. "You know what this fire means, don't you?" she cried. "It's not just our fine Capitol building that's gone. Some are wanting to move the capital of Virginia away from Williamsburg, and if that happens, we'll all be out of business and gone from here before long." She held her apron up to her face and sobbed.

Trying to catch up with John, Ann ran on, dodging around the people on the street. Her heart pounded, not from running, but because the woman had been afraid. Could the woman be right? If Williamsburg was no longer the capital, then Governor Gooch would leave, and the burgesses and the people who worked in the offices of the colonial government would leave, too. Ann's father would lose most of his patients. Would he have to move as well?

Ann didn't want to move away from Williamsburg. All of her family and friends were there, and it would break her heart to leave them.

"John!" she cried out in panic. "Wait for me!"

Chapter Two

Ann squeezed through the crowd, wriggling to John's side. For a few moments she stood silently, fascinated by the bursts of red and gold flame and the loud crackling and crunching as the fire destroyed the Capitol.

She was glad to see that no one had been hurt. If there had been injuries, her father would have been on hand, helping. If she were a doctor, she'd be helping, too. She'd carry a bag filled with bandages and splints and ointments, and she'd hurry to the side of anyone who needed aid.

As she watched the line of men hurrying to throw buckets of water on the blaze, the crowd surged forward. Ann grabbed John's arm. "John! Listen! A woman told me—"

She stopped as a gentleman who towered above her

spoke loudly, drowning out her words. "'Tis time to leave and establish a new capital elsewhere in Virginia. 'Tis clear to me the destruction of the Capitol is an omen."

A woman's voice, high-pitched with fear, said, "Aye. You're right, sir. 'Tis an omen."

Others joined in, agreeing, and Ann's heart began to pound again. She didn't want to live somewhere else in Virginia.

She tugged harder at John's arm. "Do you hear what they're saying?"

John winced and clapped a hand over his ear. "Don't yell, Ann. I can hear you."

"Then you know that—"

Someone questioned the wisdom of moving the capital, but the voices in favor of finding a new place for it were louder.

"John!" Ann shouted over the roar of the fire and the heated remarks of the bystanders. "I don't want to leave Williamsburg!"

Suddenly Matthew Davenport poked his head between Ann and John. Matthew, the thirteen-year-old brother of Ann's best friend, Peachy, grinned at Ann. "They'll move the capital without asking *your* opinion, missy," he taunted. "They'll move in the middle of the night, and you'll be asleep and get left behind."

"They will not!" Ann cried. She knew that Matthew was full of wild tales that always turned out to be untrue.

He enjoyed making up stories that would terrify his younger brothers and sisters . . . and Ann. What could he, a bossy, mean boy, possibly know about the fate of Williamsburg?

"Go away," she said to him.

Matthew just leaned closer. "Your father will have to go to the new capital, because there won't be enough people left in Williamsburg for him to doctor." He grinned. "They'll build the new capital on swampland, where there are lots of snakes. And at first they won't have enough houses for all the people, so you'll have to live in a hut with a dirt floor that will let the snakes slide in easily."

"Stop it, Matthew!" Ann cried.

She tried to edge forward in the crowd to get away from him, but a strong hand clamped down on her shoulder.

"No closer now, child," a soft voice said.

Ann whirled to see two slaves from the Geddy household, Cato and Old Betty.

White-haired Old Betty, who claimed to be older than most folk could count, smiled at her. "Look at all those sparks flyin'. You don't want them landin' on you and burnin' holes in that pretty cloak. Let's all move back and give those men carryin' buckets plenty of room."

Obediently Ann and John began to step back.

But Ann stopped and cringed against Old Betty as the cupola with its bells and clock tower tumbled onto the roof of the Capitol building with a horrifying crash. The flames shot even higher than before, covering the entire roof like a fiery curtain.

"Oh, mercy, mercy," Old Betty gasped.

"Truly an omen," a nearby woman whispered.

Ann shook her head. How could anyone possibly think this fire was an omen? She shivered and took another step back, remaining as close as possible to Old Betty.

"Do your parents know you're here, child?" Old Betty asked.

As Ann turned to answer, she saw Dr. McKenzie at the edge of the crowd. Square-shouldered, lean, and tall, her Scottish-born father strode up to the men who were directing the bucket brigade. Ann could see the relief on their faces as they spoke with him, and she felt a burst of pride. Since he was a doctor, his presence was important. He had come to help.

"There's my father now," she told Old Betty. Ann squirmed through the crowd until she could step up beside him. She tried to behave as though it were perfectly right for her to be there. "Hello, Papa," she said politely. "'Tis quite a fire. Fortunately, no one was injured."

He frowned as he saw her, but he said only, "That's what I was told, daughter."

Quickly Ann said, "If anyone had been hurt, I would have sent someone to find you, Papa. And until you arrived, I would have helped care for them. I remember what you told me—camphorated oil for burns, smelling salts for those who faint, and—"

Dr. McKenzie held out his hand. "Come with me, Ann," he said firmly.

Ann obediently put her hand into his.

As they turned to leave the scene of the fire, Ann blurted out her fears. "Some people say that the fire's an omen, but it's not, is it, Papa?"

Her father didn't answer.

"Those people want to move the capital away from Williamsburg. They won't, will they, Papa?"

Dr. McKenzie silently paced his stride to match Ann's shorter steps and continued on the path toward home.

Ann could see the exhaustion in her father's face. She knew that he'd been out most of the night with old Mr. Lynch, who was very ill.

Eager to take some of the burden from her father, she spoke up. "Papa, let me help you with your work. Take me with you when you visit the sick."

"I have taken you with me . . . at times," Dr. McKenzie answered.

Encouraged, Ann persisted. "But only at times. I want to go with you more often. You can teach me what to do. I want to help people, too."

She gave a hop over a root in the dirt path and a skip to keep up with him. "Papa," she said, "someday I will be a doctor—just like you."

They had reached their home, but Dr. McKenzie paused on the front steps. His voice was patient and soft as he said, "Ann, as you well know, this is not the time to talk of this matter. The issue at hand is your improper behavior this morning. You know as well as I do that it was not your place to be at the fire. I'll let your mother determine your punishment."

Ann gulped. She dreaded facing her mother, who wouldn't be half as understanding as her father had been. Ann took a deep breath and followed her father into the house.

When Joanna McKenzie saw what her daughter was wearing, her blue eyes snapped and she clapped her hands to her cheeks. "Running around outside in your shift!" she cried. "And no stockings or cap! What will people think?"

"Nobody knew, Mama," Ann tried to explain. "My cloak covered me from head to foot. Besides, people were looking at the fire, not at me."

"No matter," Mrs. McKenzie scolded. "Look at you, Ann! Your face needs washing, and your hair is a tangle!

No proper young lady would set foot outside her door in your condition!"

Ann meekly accepted the scolding. She realized it was a just punishment for choosing to run off with John and see the fire. But she had to admit to herself that the adventure was worth the scolding.

Finally Mrs. McKenzie's boiling temper cooled down to a simmer, like water in a kettle taken off the fire. She gave a long sigh and said, "Hurry upstairs and dress, daughter. I'll be up soon to lace your stays. We'll get a good start on the washing and then have breakfast."

Ann stiffened her body and drew her shoulders back as her mother tightened the laces of her stays. Then Ann put on her dress and apron.

Soon after her mother had left to go back downstairs, Ann followed her. Ann's clothing was tidy, and her hair was brushed and tucked neatly into a snug white cap. Her mother would find no fault now with Ann's appearance.

But as Ann made her way across the passage, she noticed that the door of her father's study stood open. Across the wood-paneled room, on a shelf of the bookpress, rested something that had always fascinated her—a human skull.

When she was little, she had wondered: *Who did this*

skull belong to? Where did it come from? One day she had asked her father.

He had pulled her onto his lap and spoken to her as he would to another adult. "I don't know to whom it belonged. I can't answer your questions, Ann."

Ann had thought a moment. Then she had asked, "Why do you keep a human skull in your bookpress, Papa?"

Dr. McKenzie had smiled. "I have an answer for that question. I keep the skull there because it's a constant reminder of the physician's need to heal. Do you understand?"

The words were long and grown-up, but Ann had seen the love and caring in her father's eyes—the same love and caring he gave his patients. She had understood.

Now, keeping her eyes on the skull, Ann entered the study. She walked directly to the skull and stretched out one finger to touch it. "When I'm a doctor, I'll own a skull exactly like this one," she said aloud.

"Nooooo you wooon't!" came a low groan that shivered up Ann's backbone.

Terrified, she jumped and let out a shriek.

Chapter Three

Matthew Davenport stumbled out from behind the study door. He doubled over with laughter.

"What are you doing in my father's study?" Ann angrily demanded.

"I came to ask him to open the apothecary early," Matthew answered. "My mother needs oil of cloves for our cook, Pegg, who's suffering a toothache. Dr. McKenzie has gone to his shop to get some for me."

Ann loved her father's shop. And she liked helping her parents and Zachary Twill, who worked sometimes in the apothecary next to their house. The small store was filled with the mingled scents of herbs and chemicals, along with the fragrances of rosewater, lavender, cinnamon, and nutmeg. Large glass jars filled the shelves along the walls. Some of the liquid contents were colorful, sparkling as they caught the morning light. Some were dark and mysterious. All were designed to heal, and Ann ached to learn how.

"Have you begun packing your things yet for the move to the new capital?" Matthew teased. "Be sure to remind your father to bring plenty of medicine for snakebite."

He lowered his voice and made one fist into what looked like the head of a snake. He hissed as he made it dart at her.

Ann jumped back, nearly colliding with her father, who had stepped into the room.

Dr. McKenzie gave a small package to Matthew, then looked down with a special smile for Ann. "Your mother is waiting for you," he said quietly.

"Yes, Papa," Ann replied. She turned, with only a polite "good-bye" to Matthew. She had intended to hurry to join her mother, but she stopped just outside the doorway as she heard Matthew speak.

"Earlier, you promised to tell me about an unusual disease you treated, sir."

"Yes, indeed, Matthew," Ann's father answered. "I'm delighted by your interest in my work."

Ann frowned at her father's response, and angry tears burned behind her eyes. "That's not fair!" she muttered. "Papa won't talk about his work with me, but he's glad to tell mean old Matthew!"

Ann threw on her cloak and burst through the back door. She ran to the large iron pot that rested over a fire.

Mrs. McKenzie took a quick, sweeping look at Ann and nodded with satisfaction. "You can help by bringing out the shifts and other linens that have been soaking overnight," she said. "The water's at the boil, so we're ready to wash them."

Just as Ann had expected, there was no trace of anger left in her mother's voice. Her mother's infrequent flashes of temper came and went like storms in the middle of summer. When the dark clouds had passed, the world quickly became a happy, sunny place once more.

As they worked, Mrs. McKenzie, curious about the fire, was full of questions for Ann. Myrtilla and Silver seemed every bit as interested and listened carefully. Ann, enjoying her audience, described in detail the horrible roar of the fire. She also repeated the comments she had heard about the possibility of moving the capital away from Williamsburg.

Myrtilla spoke up. "There's people here badly wantin' to move the capital. The young gentleman who came by this mornin' told me there's talk the fire'd been set."

Mrs. McKenzie said, "Deliberately set? Oh, dear! Who would do a terrible thing like that?"

Ann wanted to tell them that they shouldn't pay

attention to anything Matthew Davenport said. But she thought about some of the people at the fire who'd loudly argued that the capital of Virginia should be moved. Would any of them feel so strongly that they'd actually burn down their beautiful Capitol building? She shuddered.

"We may learn more this afternoon," Mrs. McKenzie said. "Remember that Margaret Davenport and her daughters, Judith and Peachy, along with Katherine Blaikley, are coming to tea. Since Joseph Davenport is town clerk, he's bound to know things the rest of us can only guess at."

Ann smiled. Peachy was her best friend, and even though their mothers would use the tea party as a way to teach their daughters the rules of social behavior, Ann was counting on an enjoyable visit. She and Peachy would sit properly, their backbones straight, their shoulders held back and down. They'd balance their tea bowls and saucers gracefully in their left hands while nibbling politely at the sweet, thin Shrewsbury cakes. And they'd remain silent, respecting the adults' right to speak without interruption.

But as soon as they'd all had their fill of the cakes, they'd ask to be excused, and that was when the fun would begin. Ann knew that Judith would take her knitting from her work bag and remain with the women. But not Peachy. She would rush upstairs with Ann to talk and giggle and hear *her* version of what had gone on at the fire.

Ann worked with her mother to ready the parlor for tea. The chairs were pulled away from the wall and set around the tea table.

As Mrs. McKenzie placed her best blue-and-white delftware teapot, tea bowls, and plates on the sideboard table, Ann clapped her hands in delight. "Oh, Mama, it looks beautiful!"

The clock chimed, and Mrs. McKenzie smiled. "Time to spruce up for tea, daughter. Our guests will be here soon."

Exactly on time, Mrs. Blaikley arrived with the Davenports. Myrtilla hung up their cloaks as Mrs. McKenzie and Ann led their guests to the parlor.

After they were seated, Mrs. McKenzie began to pour the tea. Ann knew that, as eldest daughter, it would someday be her turn to preside at the tea table. Watching how gently and carefully her mother handled the beautiful delftware, Ann was glad that she didn't have the responsibility yet.

Mrs. McKenzie politely inquired of Mrs. Blaikley, "How does your daughter, Mary? I pray she is well."

Each of the women discussed her family. Then, with the pleasantries over, Mrs. Davenport had news to tell.

"All the timber and woodwork in the Capitol were destroyed in the fire," she said. "Only the brick walls are left standing. Mr. Davenport assured me that they are in good condition, with only a few small cracks, and can easily be repaired if the Capitol is rebuilt."

Mrs. Blaikely took a small sip of tea, then asked, "What happened to all the records and important papers kept in the building? Were they lost?"

"By no means," Mrs. Davenport said. "Happily, they were all preserved, along with the pictures of the Royal Family and some other important items."

"How fortunate!" Mrs. McKenzie exclaimed. She handed a small cake to William, who was playing at her feet. Then Mrs. McKenzie looked at Ann and gave a slight nod.

Ann immediately put down her blue-and-white delftware cup, picked up the plate of cakes from the tea table, and passed it again to all the guests.

"The damage could have been even worse than it was," Mrs. Blaikley noted. "'Tis fortunate for us all that the fire didn't spread throughout the town."

"I heard that the wind shifted to the northeast, carrying the sparks away from Duke of Gloucester Street," Mrs. McKenzie said.

Mrs. Davenport lowered her voice, as though she were telling a great secret. "I have heard that the fire might have been deliberately set," she confided.

As Mrs. McKenzie and Mrs. Blaikley leaned slightly forward, Mrs. Davenport continued. "Mr. Davenport told me that Governor Gooch was informed the fire had been set. It began in an upper room without a chimney and made such rapid progress it could not have happened in any other way."

Mrs. Blaikley gave a shocked gasp. "Wicked!" she said. "What else did your husband tell you?"

"He said there is a group of people who want to establish a town on the Pamunkey River and rebuild the Capitol there."

Ann yelped, which caused her mother to look up quickly and frown.

"I'm sorry, Mama," Ann cried out. "But we can't move to the Pamunkey River and live in huts with snakes!"

Mrs. McKenzie ignored Ann's impolite outburst. She glanced at the girls' empty plates and asked quietly, "Would you young ladies like to be excused?"

"Yes, thank you, Mrs. McKenzie," Peachy said.

"Yes, thank you, Mama," Ann quickly murmured.

"Mama, cake?" William asked.

Mrs. McKenzie handed him another little cake and said, "Ann, will you girls please take William with you?"

Ann picked up her little brother, snuggling her nose into his fat baby neck.

Just as Ann had expected, Judith opened the small

work bag she had placed by her chair and pulled out her knitting.

Ann and Peachy put their tea bowls and saucers on the sideboard table and left the parlor. Once in the passage, they picked up their skirts and raced up the stairs.

As Ann gently shut the door of her bedchamber, Peachy nearly exploded with excitement. "Matthew said you were at the fire, Ann! Wearing your shift under your cloak!"

Ann felt herself blush. She hid her face by placing William on the floor and handing him a small cloth doll to play with. She hadn't thought anyone knew what she'd been wearing. Had her cloak fallen open?

"John Geddy woke me and told me about the fire," Ann explained. Peachy had already seated herself on Ann's bed, so Ann perched on the small chair. "John told me to hurry or he wouldn't wait. I didn't have time to get dressed."

Peachy lay back on the bed, laughing. "I wish I'd seen you watching a fire in nothing but your shift!"

"It wasn't like that," Ann insisted. "I was well covered. I wore my cloak over my shift."

"Surely you wore your shoes and stockings?"

"I wore my shoes, but I didn't have time for stockings," Ann answered.

Peachy laughed again, but her expression soon

changed into a look of concern. "Oh, dear. Did your parents find out? Did you get into trouble?"

"Yes," Ann said. "Mama was angry."

Peachy sadly shook her head. "Oh, Ann, you are always in a pickle. What's to become of you?"

Chapter Four

"I know what will become of me," Ann said. "Someday I will become a doctor."

"You've said this before," Peachy reminded her. "But you can't be a doctor because you're a girl. I've never heard of a woman doctor."

Suddenly Peachy's eyes widened. "You could be a midwife—like Mrs. Blaikley. Even if women can't be doctors, they certainly can be midwives. There will always be women having babies, and they'll need midwives to help them."

"That's true," Ann said. She thought about Mrs. Blaikley's job. Would it be as interesting as that of a doctor?

Peachy stared up at the ceiling. "I wonder what it's like," she said.

"Being a midwife?" Ann asked. "Well, I'm fairly sure

that a midwife's duties are to come quickly when sent for, to see to the mother's needs, and to care for the baby."

"I don't mean what's it like being a midwife," Peachy said. "I mean having a baby. What is that like?" She sat up and looked at Ann.

"I don't know," Ann said. She leaned forward in her chair. "One day, when I was seven, Papa took me to stay with Mrs. Frisk, over on Prince George Street. That evening he came to get me and told me that William had been born. I asked Mama where William had come from and how he had got here, but she just said I would know when I grew up." She sighed. "I've always been curious."

"Me too," Peachy said. "I asked my mother once, but she said it's better not to be curious. She reminded me that too much curiosity is unbecoming in a young lady."

In Ann's opinion, having a baby was a fascinating subject, one that any girl or woman would want to know about. Why should it be kept a mystery?

"When I grow up, I'm going to have babies," she said. "But first I want to know what happens."

"So do I," Peachy said.

"And if I'm going to be a midwife, I should know what midwives do," Ann added.

"You'd best talk to Mrs. Blaikley. Maybe she'll tell you," Peachy said.

"That's a good idea," Ann answered. There was so much she wondered about, so much she wanted to learn.

Ann had learned to read at a young age, and it had come quickly and easily to her. Both of her parents had been surprised at how early she could read. Now she could write and cipher—probably every bit as well as any boy could do.

"My bright little daughter," her father had called her.

Then Matthew had told her it was a known fact that women's brains were weaker than men's brains, and that women had difficulty controlling their passions, so they needed men to guide and direct them with their superior wisdom.

Indignant, Ann had gone to her father with this tale. He had admitted that this had long been the accepted point of view, but he said she shouldn't concern herself about it. There were some things that women were just not meant to do. The job women had been designed to do was to care for their families and households. It was a waste of time and energy to fight against ideas that had stood the test of time.

Ann's mother had agreed. "Someday you will marry," she'd said. "As you grow into young womanhood, I'll continue to teach you to manage a household. Believe me, Ann, dear, it's not an easy task. Running your household, managing your servants, sewing most of your family's clothing, keeping accounts, nursing the family or servants who are ill, and caring for and teaching your children will keep you busy from morning till night. All that is a woman's job, and she has been created to do it well and skillfully."

Ann knew there were other things a woman could do. Mrs. Blaikley—widowed when her one daughter was very young—had begun supporting herself and Mary with her work as a midwife. She kept account books and operated a household with four slaves.

If a woman can do these tasks, why can't she learn to use her skills in performing other jobs as well? Ann wondered.

"Ann . . . Ann," Peachy called. "Stop daydreaming."

Ann realized that she was neglecting her duties as a hostess. She should entertain her guest. "How about a game of Hide the Thimble?" she quickly asked.

"Lovely," Peachy said. She pulled a thimble from her pocket and held it up. "I'll be It. Close your eyes and count to twenty while I hide the thimble. No peeking!"

That evening, after supper, Ann sat with her parents in the parlor and knitted on a stocking. She listened quietly as they talked about the Capitol fire and the effect it might have on Williamsburg. But as Dr. McKenzie spoke of problems involved in moving his practice and his apothecary, Ann forgot herself.

"Papa, we can't go to the Pamunkey River. There aren't even any houses built yet! We can't live in a hut with snakes!"

Her father's eyes widened in surprise. "Ann, I don't know where you got a strange idea like that," he said. "We will not live in a hut. And there will be no snakes allowed in our house."

"But Matthew said . . ."

Mrs. McKenzie sighed and rolled her eyes. "We should have known. Matthew Davenport again. He seems to enjoy disturbing the younger children with wild tales." She kept her eyes on the small stocking she was knitting for William as she said, "I'm afraid the Davenport boys are not disciplined as carefully as they should be. Remember a number of years ago, when Matthew's older brother, Bedford, was reprimanded by the burgesses for writing indecent inscriptions on one of their chairs?"

"Really? What did he write?" Ann asked.

"I'm sure no one remembers now," Dr. McKenzie answered quickly. He smiled and added, "Trust me, Ann. I will do my best to take good care of you, your mother, and William for the rest of my life. Matthew was only jesting with you."

"It's not amusing," Ann grumbled. "And neither is Matthew."

"Pray don't think harshly of Matthew," Dr. McKenzie said. "He's a fine young man. He has shown an interest in my work, and it has been my pleasure to encourage him."

Before Ann could respond, Mrs. McKenzie leaned over to examine her knitting. "Dear," she said, "you dropped a stitch in this last row."

Ann groaned. "Will you tell me to pull them out and do them over?"

"It's all a part of learning," Mrs. McKenzie told her gently. "Someday you'll be grateful that you can knit well."

Ann let the stocking drop to the floor. "What good does it do to make neat stitches? Can't someone else make the stockings while I learn what I want to learn?"

"Exactly what is it that you want to learn?" her mother asked.

Even Ann's father looked up from his armchair in surprise.

"I want to learn Latin, and after that, Greek," she said. "The knowledge of Latin seems necessary to the study of medicine. I want to learn everything I'll need to know so that I can read all the books in Papa's library."

Mrs. McKenzie's expression showed that she had no patience with such a foolish wish. "Ann, you've learned to read well, and you find great pleasure in books, but the books in your father's library are beyond your abilities. They couldn't possibly interest you."

"But they do, Mama," Ann insisted. "Sometimes I take down one of Papa's medical books and read parts of it—the parts I can understand. I hope someday to know the meanings of all the words so that I can read entire books."

Mrs. McKenzie sighed. "Some of those books are not appropriate for you, daughter. There are many more useful things for you to learn. As you grow older, I hope there will be lessons for you in dancing and possibly the flute or harpsichord. And I'll continue to teach you how to manage a household."

"I'll study whatever you wish, Mama, but I still hope to study Latin and mathematics, too," Ann said.

She saw her mother give a knowing look to her father.

"Your father has greatly indulged you in taking you beyond the fundamental rules of arithmetic, in teaching you mathematics," Mrs. McKenzie told her. "But all you need is enough knowledge of arithmetic to keep your household accounts. Forget this ridiculous desire to become a doctor."

Ann took a deep breath. "Mama, Papa came to the colonies from Scotland. He once told me it was because he was searching for opportunity. Should it surprise you that I am looking for opportunity, too? Here in Virginia I should have the opportunity to study the practice of medicine."

Dr. McKenzie sighed. "It's not that simple, daughter," he said. "A woman doctor would not be accepted. We must follow custom."

"But—"

"You're an eager student, but I'm afraid the study of Latin is suitable only to young gentlemen. I'd suggest you might try harder to please your mother with the neatness of your knitting."

Ann bent down to pick up her stocking. The lump in her throat hurt. No one—not even her parents or her best friends—understood. How could she ever convince them that her life's work was to care for others?

Chapter Five

The next day Mrs. McKenzie asked Ann to run an errand. "Put on your cloak and gloves, because it's a mighty cold day," she said.

"Where do you want me to go, Mama?" Ann asked with surprise. Silver was usually asked to run errands.

Mrs. McKenzie smiled. "I made enough Shrewsbury cakes to share with the Geddy family," she said. "I'd like you to take them to Mrs. Geddy."

Ann had greedily counted on enjoying the extra cakes during the week. "Why are you giving the cakes to Mrs. Geddy?"

"It's a way of telling Anne Geddy we harbor no ill will toward John for encouraging you to steal out at dawn in order to view the Capitol fire," Mrs. McKenzie answered. "You were the one at fault, daughter, for going without permission."

Ann thought even more hungrily of the cakes. "Couldn't you just tell Mrs. Geddy this, Mama?"

"The cakes will tell her—and in a more gracious way."

"Will she understand?"

"Of course."

"I don't."

"You will when you are older and learn more of the rules of polite behavior."

As Ann sighed, her mother smiled. "You may stay and visit with the Geddys if you are invited to do so. And if they serve tea and the cakes, you may have one . . . only one."

One cake was better than no cake at all. Ann threw on her cloak and carried the covered pan of cakes down Palace Street to the Geddys' house.

Ann liked visiting the Geddys, especially when John took her to watch the workers in the foundry behind the house. The fire, the bellows, the pounding, and the sparks were a wonder to see.

Mrs. Geddy, in spite of having been widowed and left with eight children to raise just two and a half years before, was always cheerful. She gave an appreciative glance at the cakes and said, "Pray give your kind mother my heartfelt thanks. Now, let's all have some tea and these fine cakes."

After they'd eaten and Ann had played peep-boo with John's littlest sister, Sarah, Mrs. Geddy said, "I know you like to visit the foundry, Ann, so you have my permission to do so."

"Mr. Beadle won't mind?" Mr. Beadle had worked for Mr. Geddy. And after Mr. Geddy died, Mrs. Geddy had hired Mr. Beadle to run the foundry.

"Not a bit," Mrs. Geddy answered. "He's doing well, and the older boys are learning under his instruction. Someday, I hope, David and William will be able to take over their father's business. I am pleased, too, with the progress James has made in his apprenticeship with my tenant, Samuel Galt."

"Will John be an apprentice, too?" Ann asked.

"If it is John's wish, as soon as he's old enough."

"I'm old enough now, Mother," John insisted.

"I'll be the one to decide when you're old enough," Mrs. Geddy said with a chuckle. "However, if you think you're not doing enough work—"

"Come on, Ann, if you want to see the foundry," John said quickly, and dashed out the back door.

Ann hurried after him.

In the foundry she watched William Geddy help Mr. Beadle pour molten brass into a mold. On the other side of the room, she saw David Geddy bring down a hammer again and again, flattening the end of a red-hot iron rod. "Is this what you want to do when you are grown?" she asked John.

"At first I did," John said. He looked at Ann, and his

eyes gleamed. "But James has told me about some of the beautiful plates and bowls that he helps Mr. Galt make from silver. Maybe I can become a silversmith as well. I'll make silver candlesticks, and you can buy them."

Ann nodded agreement, but her heart wasn't in it. The job of silversmith seemed to be one more job that men could do but women couldn't.

A few days later Ann was given permission to visit the Davenports.

"Oh, good," Peachy said as Ann hung her cloak by the door. "Now there are enough of us for a game of whist. I'll tell Judith and Mama. They'll play with us. I'd ask Matthew to play, but he's stuck on some problems in mathematics."

"I am not stuck," Matthew called from where he sat at a small table in a room to one side of the passage.

"Mama said you were," Peachy answered. "And she said you must finish the problems before your tutor gets here."

"Be quiet. Go away!" Matthew growled.

"I'll set a table for the game," Peachy said. She went toward the dining room, but Ann walked to the table where Matthew was working and leaned over his shoulder to study his slate. "What problems can't you do?"

Matthew scowled at her. "What difference does it make if I tell you? You wouldn't know how to solve any of these problems."

"Yes, I would," Ann said. "They're vulgar fractions. Look . . . the numerator of a fraction is to be considered as a dividend, and the denominator as a divisor. If the numerator and denominator of a fraction be either both multiplied or both divided by the same number, the quotients will keep the same proportion to one another." Ann stopped to draw a breath and added, "Let me show you."

She took the chalk from Matthew's hand, picked up his slate, and demonstrated how to solve the first problem. "There," she said. "Did you see what I did? Do you want me to show you again?"

Matthew frowned. "You think you're so smart!" he snapped. "You're only a girl, and girls have weak brains, Ann McKenzie. If I can't do the problems, then neither can you."

Ann looked at him, surprised. "You just saw me do it."

"How do I know the answer is right?"

Patiently Ann said, "I'll solve the next problem, and you watch how I do it. I'll explain as I go along."

Without waiting for Matthew's answer, she solved the second problem. "Did you understand what I did?"

Matthew didn't answer. He leaned back in his chair and stared at Ann. "How did you know how to do that?"

"Papa taught me."

"It's not proper for girls to study mathematics."

"I know. Or Latin, either. That's what everyone tells me again and again."

Matthew's mouth fell open in amazement. "Do you know Latin, too?"

"No." Ann shook her head. "No one will teach me."

Matthew slid upright in his chair. His eyes gleamed, and his lips parted in a smile. "I will," he said.

Ann gasped. "You will? Really? Truly?"

"Yes, I will," Matthew said. "I'll make a bargain with you. If you'll do my mathematics problems for me, I'll teach you Latin."

Surprised, Ann asked, "Wouldn't you rather just learn to solve the problems?"

Matthew grinned. "I'll learn sooner or later. For now it would suit me best if you did them for me."

"You'll really teach me Latin?"

"Absolutely. I promise."

"Agreed!" Ann cried.

Peachy stepped into the room. "I heard what you said, Matthew. Ann can't do your problems for you. It's not fair."

"Not fair to whom?" Matthew asked. "It's fair to me,

41

and it's fair to Ann. She'll learn Latin, which is something she wants to do."

"It's not fair to your tutor," Peachy insisted. She turned to Ann and complained, "Ann, you'll be helping Matthew trick his tutor."

Ann could hardly believe that soon she was going to learn Latin. "Matthew will soon learn the way to solve these problems, and I'll learn Latin," she told Peachy. "No one will be harmed."

"Well . . ." Peachy looked dubious.

"Please don't tell on us," Ann begged her friend. "Let Matthew teach me. You don't know how much I want to learn Latin. No one else will teach me—not even Papa."

"If you tell anyone that I'm teaching Ann Latin, you'll spoil Ann's secret, and it *must* be kept secret," Matthew said.

Peachy nodded. "I'll keep your secret, Ann," she said.

Matthew chuckled. *"Prima caritas incipit a se ipso,"* he said to Ann.

Ann stared at him. "What did you say?"

"I said, 'Thank you very much,'" Matthew said. His eyes twinkled. "That's Latin."

"Prima caritas incipit a se ipso," Ann repeated slowly. She liked the smooth, rounded feel of the words on her tongue. *"Prima caritas incipit a se ipso."*

"That's it," Matthew said. He handed Ann the slate.

"You must hurry if you're going to finish these problems before my tutor arrives."

Ann took the slate. "Tell the others I'll be with them in a minute," she said to Peachy.

As Peachy left, Ann bent to the table, next to Matthew. "You should watch me," she said, "so that you'll learn."

Matthew leaned away from her and made a shooing motion with his hands. "We haven't time for all that," he said. "Just do the problems."

Ann nodded, but she paused. "When will we begin the Latin lessons?"

"We'll think about that later," Matthew said. He jumped up, moved away from the table, and pointed to the chair. "Hurry up, Ann. My tutor will soon be here. Get busy."

It took Ann only a few minutes to finish solving the problems. She could have solved them even more quickly if Matthew had sat still instead of pacing back and forth across the room.

Now and then he'd stop to look over her shoulder.

"Do you want to learn how I—" Ann began.

But Matthew nervously exclaimed, "There's no time! Hurry!"

As Ann was finishing the last problem, a loud knock on the front door made her jump.

"There he is! Give me the slate! Be quick about it!"

Matthew cried. He grabbed the slate from her hands, then pulled her from the chair and pushed her into the passage.

Ann scurried out of the way as Matthew opened the door to admit a thin, spindly-legged young man. George Dunn! Ann recognized him immediately. She had seen him in her father's apothecary shop and knew he was a student at the College of William and Mary. Suddenly she realized that Matthew's trick wouldn't be played on a nameless, faceless "tutor," but on George Dunn—a real person who had always been courteous to her.

Her face burning, Ann lowered her eyes and curtsied.

"Miss McKenzie," Mr. Dunn said, acknowledging her curtsy with a bow. "You are looking well."

"Prima caritas incipit a se ipso," Ann answered.

Mr. Dunn's eyebrows shot up. "I beg your pardon?" he asked.

Matthew quickly interrupted. He stepped between Ann and Mr. Dunn and held out his slate. "Here are the problems I've solved. I think you'll find they're all correct."

Mr. Dunn glanced at the slate. "Well done, Master Davenport," he said.

As Matthew took Mr. Dunn's arm, propelling him into the library, Ann didn't wait to hear any more. She shouldn't have spoken in Latin. Not yet. It was too soon to give away her secret. Her heart thumping, she fled down the passage to the room where Peachy was waiting.

Ann greeted Mrs. Davenport and Judith, who looked up from her chair at the small table. "We've been waiting for you, Ann," Judith said.

"Never mind," Peachy said quickly. "Ann's finally here. Deal the cards, Judith."

Ann loved the game of whist and loved winning, which she and her partner often did. But today she played badly, even trumping her partner's ace.

"Ann!" Peachy said loudly. "Wake up! It's your turn to deal."

"Oh," Ann murmured. "I'm sorry." She snatched up the deck of cards. She began to shuffle them, but they slipped through her fingers, scattering across the table.

Judith sighed impatiently.

Peachy looked into Ann's eyes. "You don't have to do it," she said. Ann knew Peachy meant she didn't have to help Matthew. But the others didn't know.

"Ann, dear," Mrs. Davenport said, "if you don't want to deal, I'll be happy to do it for you."

"No, thank you, Mrs. Davenport," Ann said. As she turned to Peachy, her voice was firm. "I *am* going to do it, Peachy. I've made up my mind."

"I don't want you to get into trouble."

"What's the matter with you, Peachy?" Judith asked.

"Ann's not going to get into trouble because she dropped the cards."

"There's not going to be any trouble," Ann said, and hoped she was right. She gathered the cards, shuffled the deck, and dealt.

Chapter Six

During the month of February, when she wasn't help-ing in the apothecary or entertaining William, Ann spent most afternoons at the Davenports' home, each time doing Matthew's mathematics lessons for him. In return, he taught her Latin phrases, which she repeated over and over, memorizing them.

One Saturday morning in early March, as Ann's fam-ily was finishing breakfast, Myrtilla came into the din-ing room. "Dr. McKenzie," she said. "The Pegrams over on Francis Street just sent word, askin' you to come. Their youngest boy's been sufferin' from earache all night."

"Thank you, Myrtilla," Dr. McKenzie said. He touched his napkin to his lips, then added, "Will you please send Silver to request Mr. Twill's assistance in the apothecary this morning?"

As Dr. McKenzie pushed back his chair, he said to Mrs. McKenzie, "Old Henry Davis has been bothered lately with a hoarseness that refuses to leave. I think I'll stop by and visit him, too."

Ann stopped spoon-feeding gruel to William and jumped to her feet. "Papa," she begged, "will you take me with you? I can help you."

Mrs. McKenzie answered for him. "Your father won't need your help. Surely the Pegrams and Davises will have family on hand, if help should be needed."

"But, Papa, this will give me another chance to watch you work," Ann said.

"Dear daughter," Mrs. McKenzie said, "you must put out of your mind this notion that you might someday be a doctor. It will not happen. We've already told you there's not even a small possibility."

Ann looked at her father pleadingly.

He put a hand on her shoulder and smiled. "It's a pleasant day, and I would like Ann's company," he said to Mrs. McKenzie. "There's no harm if she accompanies me, is there?"

"Well, I suppose no real harm, but—"

Ann didn't give her mother a chance to finish. "I'll get my cloak!" she cried, and dashed from the room.

The Pegrams lived not far from the McKenzies. The sun was warm enough to cut the early-March chill, and

Ann delighted in the shoots of daffodils that poked through the earth. She bounced along next to her father.

When they reached the Pegrams' small, two-room house, Ann could hear the exhausted wails of a small child. Other young voices were raised in an argument. As Dr. McKenzie knocked at the door, Ann heard a shriek, followed by loud sobbing.

The door flew open, and a woman, with a wailing toddler in her arms, cried, "Hush, children! The doctor's here!"

Dr. McKenzie didn't stop to introduce Ann. He stepped over the threshold and took the child from his mother.

Mrs. Pegram wiped her hands on her soiled apron and tried to tuck wisps of hair back inside her cap. She turned to the little girl who sat on the floor sobbing, her nose dripping as much as her eyes. Next to her crouched a scowling boy not more than a year older than his sister.

"You two stop your squabbling! And be quiet! Do you hear me?" Mrs. Pegram commanded.

She turned to Dr. McKenzie. "Baby Hugh's been crying most of the night. It has almost wore me out."

The little girl on the floor let out another sob. Ann wanted to watch her father, but someone had to care for Mrs. Pegram's other children. Quickly Ann sat beside them and pulled the little girl onto her lap, cuddling her until she quieted.

"You're such a fine, big boy," she said to the other child. "What's your name?"

"Frank," he answered.

"And what's your sister's name?"

"Margaret."

"I can see that you're strong, Frank, and helpful," Ann said. "I wonder if you're a big enough boy to bring me a cup of water and a small cloth."

Frank scrambled to his feet. He stood tall, puffing out his chest. "I'm big," he said. "I can get the water."

Margaret's sobs stopped completely, and she watched her brother from the shelter of Ann's lap.

Frank carried the tin cup to Ann, sloshing only a small amount of water over its sides. He ran from the room and came back with a small towel.

"What a good, helpful boy you are, Frank," Ann said.

Margaret looked up at Ann. "Frank pushed me. He made me cry," she complained.

"He won't do it again," Ann told her. "You're his little sister, and he'll take care of you. See how kind he was. He brought you water to drink."

Margaret immediately opened her mouth, but Ann said, "First we're going to clean your face."

She dipped one end of the towel in the water,

squeezed it out, and gently mopped Margaret's face. When it was clean, Ann took the other end of the towel and patted Margaret's face dry.

As Ann helped Margaret drink from the cup, she noticed that the baby had stopped crying and was nestled against his mother, sucking his thumb. Ann remembered that when her brother, William, had an earache, their father had added camphor and menthol to oil, heated the mixture, and put two drops into William's ear. Then he'd plugged it with a wad of cotton. The warmth and the extracts had taken away the pain, and William had stopped crying.

She listened as Dr. McKenzie explained to Mrs. Pegram how and when she should continue to give Hugh the warmed drops of oil. Mrs. Pegram seemed calm now, but Ann could see the exhaustion in her face as she tried to pay close attention.

Dr. McKenzie didn't rise to leave. He asked, "Is there someone who can help you with the children, madam?"

Mrs. Pegram hesitated. "Perchance my friend Mrs. Bradford, who lives two doors to the south," she said. "But since I am not ill—"

"You will soon lose your strength and become ill if you do not get some sleep," Dr. McKenzie said. He pointed to Hugh, who was already nodding off in his mother's arms. "As a doctor, I am telling you to sleep when your baby sleeps. You will wake refreshed and be much better able to care for him and for your other children."

A grateful smile flickered on Mrs. Pegram's lips.

Dr. McKenzie added, "I will call upon Mrs. Bradford and tell her of your need."

Ann said good-bye to the children and to Mrs. Pegram, who thanked her and her father profusely. Then Ann followed her father to Mrs. Bradford's doorstep, where he asked assistance for her neighbor.

As they walked toward Henry Davis's house, Dr. McKenzie smiled down at Ann. "You were a fine help to me, daughter. I'm proud of you. You calmed the crying children. You made it possible for me to give my full attention to my job of helping Mrs. Pegram's baby."

Ann felt warmed by her father's praise. She laughed as she answered, "Margaret's wailing hurt my ears. I had to do something."

Taking her father's hand as they walked up Botetourt Street to Duke of Gloucester, Ann added, "What I really wanted to do, Papa, was watch you so I could learn how to treat an earache."

Dr. McKenzie chuckled. "You can watch and learn when we visit Mr. Davis. There will be no children in the house to distract you."

Ann stayed close to her father's side as they entered

the Davises' house, which like the Pegrams' had only two rooms. Mrs. Davis led them into a bedchamber in which an elderly man sat in bed, propped up by pillows.

Even after Ann pulled off her cloak, she was still uncomfortable. The room was hot and smoky from the fireplace, and there was an ugly smell of sweat and grease.

The moment Mr. Davis spied the doctor, his eyes brightened. But his face soon sagged into an expression of misery. "The cough lingers," he complained. "At times it seems to tear out my chest. Can nothing be done about it?"

Dr. McKenzie glanced around the small bedchamber before he sat on the ladder-backed wooden chair next to the bed. "It is very warm in here," he said.

Mr. Davis nodded with such vigor that the loose skin of his jowls quivered. "I can't abide too much cold," he said.

Gently Dr. McKenzie said, "I advised you to get plenty of fresh air each day, sir."

"But it's March. It's winter. It's cold outside."

"It's cool today, not too cold. Cool air is good for the lungs."

Mr. Davis began to pout. "I'm an old man. I can't abide fresh air."

"Have you followed the instructions I gave you the

last time I was here?" Dr. McKenzie asked. "A light diet, with boiled chicken and wine to strengthen you?"

Mr. Davis's only response was a strangling sound in his throat, but Mrs. Davis spoke up.

"He has not done what you told him, Dr. McKenzie. Each day he demands his boiled beef, his beer or cider, and his pudding."

"To keep up my strength," Mr. Davis insisted.

Dr. McKenzie continued, "Do you wash each day with cold water and keep your feet clean?"

Ann wondered why he bothered to ask. The horrible odor in the room answered the question.

Mr. Davis seemed to sink lower in the bed. "I'm an old man," he mumbled, "with a terrible cough."

With that he let loose a loud, rattling cough that shook his bed. From somewhere inside his pile of pillows he pulled a large, stained rag and hacked until a lump of mucus flew into it.

Sickened, Ann closed her eyes and turned away. She wanted to run from the room but knew she couldn't—not when she had pleaded so hard to be allowed to come.

Dr. McKenzie drew a small bottle from his bag and handed it to Mrs. Davis. "I've brought you some syrup of horehound," he said to Mr. Davis. "Each night, before bedtime, your wife can make you a cup of tea and stir in a teaspoon of the syrup."

Mr. Davis rubbed his hands and smiled, showing the many gaps where his teeth were missing. "I do like that syrup of horehound," he said.

"Madam," Dr. McKenzie said to Mrs. Davis, "your husband is to have the tea only if he has spent at least half an hour outside, where he is to walk and breathe in the fresh air."

"Yes, sir," Mrs. Davis said.

"And only after he has washed," Dr. McKenzie added.

Mrs. Davis's eyes twinkled. "It will be as you say, Dr. McKenzie."

As Ann and her father left the Davises' house and walked toward home, Ann said, "Papa, Mr. Davis didn't do any of the things you'd told him he'd have to do to get well when you were there before."

"That is true," Dr. McKenzie answered.

"Do you think he'll obey your rules now, just to get the syrup of horehound in his tea?"

"Probably not."

"Then why did you bother to give it to him?"

"My job is to do my best to heal, not judge my patients," Dr. McKenzie said. "There will always be some people who do nothing to help themselves regain good health, but I must still do my best for them."

With a burst of pride Ann skipped to catch up to her father and hugged his arm. There was much for her to learn, but she had the best teacher anyone could ask for.

Chapter Seven

In a speech to the General Assembly on March 30, Governor William Gooch spoke angrily about the origin of the Capitol fire and turned rumors into fact. That night, after dinner, Dr. McKenzie told Ann and her mother about the speech.

"I must indeed own it is difficult to comprehend how such a crime could be committed, or even imagined, by any rational creature," the governor had said. Dr. McKenzie told them that the governor had gone on to explain what most people had already heard—that the fire had begun in an upper room with no chimney, and that the first persons on the scene had discovered that the entire inside of the roof was ablaze with so large a fire that it could not be extinguished.

"A fire kindled by accident could not have made so rapid a progress," Governor Gooch had continued.

"You will be forced to ascribe it to the horrid machinations of desperate villains, instigated by infernal madness."

"Do they know who set the fire?" Ann asked her father.

Dr. McKenzie shook his head. His expression was serious, but Ann could hear the humor behind his words as he said, "We do know that it couldn't have been anyone from the Colony of Virginia.'"

"How do we know that?" Ann asked.

Her father smiled as he answered, "Because the governor announced that he was sure 'such superlative wickedness could never get admittance into the heart of a Virginian.'"

Ann giggled, but she soon became serious. "Will the burgesses move the capital away from Williamsburg?"

"We can only wait and see," he said. "The House of Burgesses and the Council must agree."

Ann glanced around the parlor, with its cheerful whitewashed walls and paneled wainscot. "Papa," she said, "I like living in Williamsburg. I don't want to leave and live on the Pamunkey River."

"Nor do I," he said. "But the choice is not ours."

"It should be!" Ann burst out. "I want to choose where we live, not have someone else decide for us!"

Dr. McKenzie smiled and shook his head. "Dear daughter," he said, "you will find little support for your rebellious nature. It's better for you to learn to make the best of things. Do you understand?"

"Yes, Papa," Ann said dutifully. But she couldn't help wondering, *Why?*

During April and May, Ann often asked her father to take her with him when he visited the ill. Twice he allowed her to go. Ann cut peonies from her own garden to take to her father's patients. Williamsburg's gardens were abloom beyond their low boxwood hedges, overflowing with forget-me-nots, irises, and Cherokee roses. Shrubs glistened with new leaves, some of them—like the mountain laurel—bursting into flower.

But on the last day of May, when Myrtilla brought Dr. McKenzie a message at the breakfast table, he shook his head firmly.

"You will not come with me today, daughter. I'm discovering too many cases of smallpox," he said. "Unfortunately, the disease is spreading more rapidly than usual in this part of the colony, and I don't want to risk your catching it." He looked at Mrs. McKenzie. "It would be best if you and the children avoided crowded places."

Curious, Ann spoke up. "How would we catch the pox, Papa?"

"By coming into close contact with someone who

has it," he answered. "If you touch the sores—or even clothes or blankets that have touched the pustules—you will get the disease, too."

"But what about *you*?" Ann asked, worried. "As a doctor you come into contact with them. Is there nothing that can protect you from the pox?"

To Ann's surprise, her father nodded. "There is something called inoculation. It has been used in Africa and Asia in various forms for hundreds of years, but it did not become known here in the colonies until about twenty years ago."

"What is inoculation? What does it mean?"

"If I were to be inoculated, I would open a cut on my arm and place pus from someone else's smallpox sore into the cut. Then I would bandage it tightly and wait for the disease to take hold. I would be sick, but not as sick as someone who contracted the pox by accident. And when I recovered, I would be immune to the disease."

Ann gasped. It sounded like a dreadful thing to do. "Will you be inoculated, Papa?"

"No." Dr. McKenzie shook his head. "Some doctors in Virginia favor inoculations, but I do not because of a serious problem they cause. If I were inoculated, I would remain contagious while the disease ran its course. Anyone catching the pox from me would get it in its worst form. That means you, William, your mother, our servants, and anyone who might come into contact with me. It would also keep me from caring for my patients who became ill."

He pushed back his chair. "Now I must hurry. I suspect, from the message I received, that Mr. Davis has come down with pleurisy."

"Poor Mr. Davis," Mrs. McKenzie said.

Poor *Mrs.* Davis, Ann thought. Her sympathies were with the woman who must care for that miserable man.

Ann saw her mother gaze at her husband with concern. "Do be careful, Kenneth," she said.

"I am always careful, madam," he said with a smile. "I assure you that I have nothing to fear from Mr. Davis—other than a disagreeable disposition. And that is not contagious."

After her father had left, Ann did her household chores. She helped her mother salt the meat they had bought that morning at market. Then, under her mother's direction, she mixed the batter for a yeast bread.

"Do you need to add a bit more flour?" Mrs. McKenzie asked as she watched Ann beat the mixture. "The batter should be stiff enough for a spoon to stand in."

"Why must I learn to make bread?" Ann asked.

"Perhaps just a pinch . . . What's that? Why must you learn to make bread? Ann, you know the answer.

Someday you will cook for your husband and children."

"But I'll have slaves or servants who will do most of the cooking. Why must *I* know how to make bread?"

"Because as you manage the household, it will be your responsibility to ensure that the meals are cooked properly." Mrs. McKenzie sighed. "Good gracious, Ann. Your task is to learn to bake the bread, not ask foolish questions."

"I don't think the question is foolish, Mama," Ann answered. "Don't you ever wonder why women are obliged to do the things they must do?"

"Spoon the batter into the mold," Mrs. McKenzie said firmly. "I've greased it for you." She waited until Ann had finished and had put the mold in a warm spot near the fireplace so that the mixture could rise before baking. Then she said, "Daughter, we have spoken on many occasions about the need for a young woman to learn housewifery. You must know how to cook and run a household if you are to be a good wife."

Ann sat patiently, her eyes downcast, as her mother again explained that marriage was every young woman's natural destiny, and that her duty, as Ann's mother, was to prepare Ann to be a good wife and mother.

"And doctor," Ann whispered under her breath.

But her mother had heard her. "You cannot do both jobs," she said firmly.

"Mrs. Blaikley does. Think of the wonderful work she does in bringing babies into the world."

"Mrs. Blaikley works as a midwife because she is widowed," Mrs. McKenzie answered. "She did not remarry, so she does not have a husband to care for her."

"Maybe she didn't want another husband. Maybe she'd rather be a midwife."

"Every woman wants a husband," Mrs. McKenzie insisted.

"Like Mr. Davis?" Ann asked. "I don't think Mrs. Davis would agree."

Mrs. McKenzie's mouth twitched, and Ann could see that she was trying not to smile. "Mr. and Mrs. Davis were young once. He was not always a difficult old man." Her voice softened as she added, "Remember, Ann, the marriage vows say 'in sickness and in health.' It is a wife's duty to nurse her husband when he is ill. Just pay heed to your mother's good advice and learn to do your tasks well." She waited for Ann's response.

"Yes, Mama," Ann said quietly. She didn't want to make her mother unhappy, so she could give no other answer.

Ann worked on sewing flat-felled seams on a new linen shift. She had learned from experience that her stitches must be both closely spaced and tiny. Each week the shifts were washed in boiling water, and the stitches must hold.

It wasn't until after the afternoon meal that Ann was free to choose her own activity. Her father had gone to work in the apothecary, so Ann ran quickly to the bookshelves in her father's study. Some of his medical volumes were written in Latin. She opened a thick leather-bound book and tried to find words or phrases she recognized, but nothing looked familiar. If only she had a more learned teacher than Matthew. She sighed. Well, Matthew was better than no teacher at all.

"Ann?" Mrs. McKenzie spoke from the open doorway. "What are you doing with your father's books?"

Ann gave a start. "Just looking at them," she said quickly as she replaced the book she was holding.

"Those books will hold no interest for you," Mrs. McKenzie said. "'Tis best that you read Bickham's *Fables and Other Short Poems* or *A Private Tutor for Little Masters and Misses.* Where have you put them?"

"In my bedchamber, Mama," Ann answered. *Someday I'll be able to read Papa's books in Latin,* she thought, but she wasn't about to tell her mother that.

As Ann joined her mother in the passage, Mrs. McKenzie said, "Myrtilla and Silver are both occupied. I promised Mrs. Blaikley I'd send her a length of cloth. Will you carry it to her for me?"

"Of course I will, Mama," Ann said. She took the package from her mother.

Mrs. McKenzie smiled as Ann hugged her and ran toward the front door. "You're forgetting your hat, Ann!" she called.

Ann hurried to her room, tied on her straw hat, and dashed outside. It was the last day of May—almost June—and it was much too warm for a cloak. The yards and window boxes along the way were filled with fragrant flowers of every color.

Ann happily greeted some of the neighbors who were out-of-doors and hummed to herself as she walked to the Blaikleys' house.

Lucy, Mrs. Blaikley's house slave, opened the door and invited Ann to come inside. Lucy suddenly reached out to steady herself on the back of a chair in the passage. For an instant she closed her eyes.

"Are you not well?" Ann asked.

"It was the fish we had for supper last night," Lucy said. "Beck and Sal are down in bed. They feel even worse than I do."

"I'm sorry," Ann told her. "Is there anything I can do to help you? Do you need some medication to stop the nausea?"

"No. Bestest to get it out of the system," Lucy answered. She turned and hurried down the passage and out the back door.

Mrs. Blaikley came into the room and took the package from Ann. "Pray thank your mother for me, Ann," she said.

Ann walked with Mrs. Blaikley out to the front steps just as a small boy ran toward them. He dropped to the top step and gasped for breath. "My . . . mother . . . She sent me. . . . The baby . . . is ready to come."

"'Tis Tommy Fox, isn't it?" Mrs. Blaikley asked.

"Yes, ma'am. I'm Tommy," the boy said as he got to his feet. "My mother needs you."

"Who is with her?"

"No one. The neighbor who was supposed to help is down with the smallpox. Mama's sister, Aunt Sally, is traveling down from Richmond, but she don't know the baby's ready to get here. Mama says Aunt Sally won't come in time."

"Hurry home to your mother, Tommy," Mrs. Blaikley said. "Tell her I'll be there within a few minutes."

As Tommy ran off, Mrs. Blaikley frowned. "Oh, dear," she said. "Two of my slaves are ill, and Lucy is tending them. Anthony is out running errands. Where am I going to find someone to assist me?"

Ann's heart beat loudly. In her excitement she shouted, "I'll help you, Mrs. Blaikley!"

"No, Ann. Thank you, but . . ." Mrs. Blaikley stopped and studied Ann as she spoke to herself.

"Giving birth is nothing new for Mrs. Fox. This should be a quick and easy one. I can certainly handle it myself, but someone should be there who can keep the children busy, so they won't be underfoot."

Ann sucked in her breath. This was her chance to learn what Mrs. Blaikley did as a midwife. "I'll come with you," she said eagerly. "I can help you with anything you need. I've done this for my father."

"All right," Mrs. Blaikley agreed. "I'll tell Lucy where I've gone." She disappeared back inside her house.

Ann hopped down the steps and clapped her hands in excitement. "My first lesson as a midwife!" she cried.

Chapter Eight

There was no sign of Mr. Fox in the two-room house as Ann followed Mrs. Blaikley inside.

As she glanced quickly into the bedchamber, Tommy seemed to know what she was thinking. "Papa's not at home. He's at work at the blacksmith shop," he said.

From the bedchamber Mrs. Fox called, "Is that you, Mrs. Blaikley?"

"I'm here, dear," Mrs. Blaikley answered. She took off her hat and gloves. "We'll soon have you well taken care of." *Her voice is as strong and comforting as Papa's,* Ann noted. She would have to remember that—and practice sounding the same way.

"Hurry!" Mrs. Fox cried out. She seemed to be in pain.

Startled, Ann looked at Mrs. Blaikley, as did Mrs. Fox's children. But Mrs. Blaikley picked up the small bag she had brought with her and said, "Tend to the children, Ann." She stepped into the bedchamber and closed the door behind her.

Mrs. Fox cried out even more loudly. Ann shuddered. Was pain a part of childbirth?

Mrs. Blaikley opened the bedroom door and leaned out. "Ann, will you please put the kettle on the fire?" she asked. "The baby is almost here. Before long we'll be wanting a nice cup of tea."

Ann sent Tommy to the woodpile for wood while she filled the kettle with water. When Tommy returned, Ann put the logs on the fire dogs in the fireplace and hung the kettle on the swinging metal arm over the fire.

When she turned from the fireplace, the small, frightened faces looking up at her made her remember just why she was there. "Would you like to play Button, Button, Who's Got the Button?" she asked.

The children stared at her. None of them spoke.

"I know what we can do. We can sing," Ann said. She immediately began one of the hymns she thought everyone knew.

It didn't take long before she realized that hers was the only voice raised in song.

Two of the children stared at the closed doorway as Mrs. Fox cried out again. "Mama," the smallest boy whimpered.

"Everyone sit down on the floor with me," Ann

ordered. As the children obeyed, she gathered them close together. "I'm going to tell you a story," she said. She leaned toward the smallest boy, who was still whimpering, and asked, "What would you like the story to be about?"

The child didn't answer, but Tommy suddenly became interested. "Tell about pirates on the high seas," he said.

"Very well," Ann answered, although she wondered what in the world to put into her story. She knew very little about pirates and nothing about the high seas.

A baby's wail stopped Ann short. She jumped to her feet with the children and faced the door.

Within a few minutes, Mrs. Blaikley opened the door and smiled. "Children," she said, "you have a new baby sister. You'll be able to see her in a short while."

She turned to Ann. "Mrs. Fox and I would certainly enjoy those cups of tea now."

Ann ran to the fire and removed the kettle. She'd forgotten all about it, but luckily the water hadn't all boiled away.

Tommy found a box of tea leaves and a teapot, and Ann made the tea. Her mother had told her that brewing tea was something every woman should know how to do properly, and at least in this matter she had been right.

Ann located the other things she needed and set a

tray with two cups, a filled teapot, a bowl of sugar, and a small pitcher of milk. Tommy knocked on the bedchamber door. When Mrs. Blaikley opened it, Ann handed her the tray.

"Thank you, Ann," Mrs. Blaikley said. Then she told the children, "You may all come in and see your mother and the baby."

With excited shouts, they raced into the room to snuggle against their mother and get a good look at their new sister, who lay wrapped in a blanket in their mother's arms.

Mrs. Fox had hugs and smiles for them all. Then she glanced up at Ann. "That's a pretty name, Ann," she said. "My husband told me to think of a name for this little one. I had in mind many fine names if the baby were to be a boy, but not one for a girl. I believe I'll have her baptized Ann, after you, who so kindly helped care for my other children."

Ann beamed with pleasure. A baby named after her! What a wonderful honor! She was even more excited, though, to see this baby who was only a few minutes old.

A short time later Mrs. Fox's sister arrived. Mrs. Blaikley packed her things, and she and Ann left to walk home. It was then that it occurred to Ann that she hadn't learned a thing about how babies were born or what a midwife needed to do.

"Why was Mrs. Fox crying out in pain?" Ann asked. "What is it like to have a baby?"

Mrs. Blaikley stopped at the cross street. "This is a question you can someday ask your mother, Ann."

"But I—"

"Here is where our ways part," Mrs. Blaikley said. She patted Ann's shoulder. "Thank you again for your good help. I don't know what I would have done with all those poor dear children underfoot."

"Mrs. Blaikley, you didn't answer my question," Ann persisted.

"No, I didn't, and I'm not about to," Mrs. Blaikley told her. "You are too young now to bother your head with questions like those. Besides, it's teatime. Hurry on home so your mother won't worry about you."

Mrs. Blaikley turned the corner and strode down the street.

As Ann walked toward home, she thought about what Mrs. Blaikley had done. She had immediately taken charge in a calm, caring way. She had then gone in to help Mrs. Fox. Even though what she had done for Mrs. Fox was still a mystery to Ann, she had seen the woman's happiness with her baby and knew that Mrs. Blaikley had helped to make that happen. Maybe being a midwife would be even more interesting than being a doctor. *Maybe I can be both!* Ann thought, skipping along the path.

At home Ann found her mother folding the bed linens, smoothing them into neatly folded piles and stacking them in the linen press. Ann told her about going with Mrs. Blaikley and caring for Mrs. Fox's children.

Mrs. McKenzie frowned slightly, but she picked up a fresh stack of linens and smiled at Ann. "I'm glad you were there to help," she said. "Katherine Blaikley would never have asked you to come with her if there had been any other way."

"Mama," Ann said, "may I ask you a question?"

"Of course," Mrs. McKenzie replied. "What do you wish to know?"

"I want to know about having babies," Ann said. "What is it like?"

Mrs. McKenzie shoved the bed linens onto the shelf, then turned to Ann. "Dear child," she said, "you are only beginning to learn about a wife's responsibilities. When you are older, you will understand that childbirth is part of the joys and sorrows of motherhood."

Was this the only kind of answer anyone was going to give her?

Chapter Nine

On the first Sunday in June, close to eleven o'clock, Ann and her family walked two blocks down Palace Street to Bruton Parish Church. Attendance at Sunday services at least once a month was required by law, and most of the people in Williamsburg appeared to be there this day.

Ann loved visiting with her friends and their families each Sunday. She also loved the service, with its prayers and music. Her only problem was that sometimes her mind drifted when the Reverend Mr. Dawson's sermons became too long.

As Ann's parents stopped to chat with neighbors in the churchyard before the service, Matthew stepped up to Ann. "Come with me," he said in a low voice. "I have something important to tell you."

Curious, Ann followed him a few steps into the

cemetery. Matthew stopped beside one of the tombs. "Some of the slaves from town and some from the plantations are going to gather tonight out in Waller's Grove," he said. "There will be dancing."

"Dancing?" Ann blurted out before she could stop herself from reacting like an eager child to Matthew's news.

Matthew looked smug. "That's what I said. Dancing . . . and drums."

He waited for Ann to react again, but she tried to keep from showing her excitement. It was against the law for slaves to gather by themselves in large groups. Many white people feared that the slaves would plan a revolt. Some people also mistrusted the drums, fearing they would remind the slaves of the music of their native countries and cause them to become restless and run away.

But Ann had heard that the slaves occasionally assembled secretly on Sundays, one of the few days on which they were allowed any free time. They met hoping that slave patrols wouldn't arrive to break up the gatherings. All the slaves who could—young and old, from the town and from the plantations around Williamsburg—went to the gatherings.

Once, Ann had asked her father about the rumors. Dr. McKenzie had told her that most of the gatherings he had heard about had not led to trouble. He suspected that Myrtilla and Silver sometimes went. He even thought that they went about their tasks more willingly after they had slipped away to spend a few hours with friends and kin.

"I wonder if Myrtilla will be there," Ann said to Matthew.

"*I* will be," Matthew announced.

Ann gasped in surprise. "You can't!" she said. "The slaves will never let you."

"They won't know we're there. We'll hide. We're just going to watch."

"We? Who's 'we'?"

"John Geddy's going with me."

"You'll both get into trouble."

"No, we won't. No one caught us when we went last month."

"You really went? No! I don't believe you."

"We did. Ask John." Matthew paused. He studied Ann, then said, "Too bad you're a girl and can't go with us."

Indignantly Ann demanded, "What does being a girl have to do with it?"

"Oh, you know," Matthew said. He smiled teasingly. "Girls aren't brave enough to do something like this."

Ann clenched her teeth and scowled at Matthew. This was a frolic she'd love to see, but he said she couldn't. Just because she was a girl?

"Our parents would never allow any of us to go to a slave gathering," Matthew added. "But a girl especially can't. It's one thing to sneak out in the morning to watch the Capitol burn. It's another to sneak out *at night* to see a secret gathering."

Ann thought for only a moment. Surely it was no more harmful to watch the slaves dance than it had been to watch the dancers at last year's Christmas ball hosted by her parents.

Ann had sat for what felt like an hour watching couples dance the minuet. The dance was the most boring thing she had ever seen, with the dancers' arms held just so and toes pointed just so. The country dances were more interesting, but the slaves' dances sounded like even more fun.

Matthew lowered his voice. "Maybe if you sneaked out and watched for a while and then hurried back to bed . . . Of course, being a girl you'd be afraid."

Ann made a quick decision. "I'm not afraid," she said. "I'll go to the dance, too."

Matthew grinned. "Are you sure?"

"Yes."

"I'll tell Peachy. If you'll go, then maybe she'll want to come, too. We'll meet outside the apothecary at nine o'clock." Matthew turned and hurried away.

Ann slowly walked back to join her parents, a little frightened at her bold decision. Her stomach hurt, and there was a tightness in her chest. But she had told Matthew she was going, so she'd go. There was no turning back.

During the service, Ann's thoughts were on the evening ahead, so she had a hard time sitting still and keeping her mind on the long sermon. What she did hear made her so uncomfortable that she squirmed until her mother gave her knee a sharp tap. Mr. Dawson's thunderous words about the sinfulness of deceit seemed to be aimed directly at Ann.

I'm not deceiving anyone by going to watch the slaves dance, she reminded herself. *It's not as though Mama and Papa ever told me I couldn't go. I'll watch the dance for a little while, then go right back home to bed.*

After the service was over, Ann's father became involved in a long discussion with some of the other men. Ann overheard them talking about smallpox and the spreading epidemic, but her mind was on the slaves' gathering.

She jumped as an arm was flung around her shoulders and Peachy whispered in her ear, "Will you really go to the slave dance tonight?"

"Yes," Ann said.

Peachy giggled. "If you'll go, then I'll go, too."

Ann let out a sigh of relief. She was surprised how glad she felt to have Peachy in this adventure with her. "There's nothing wrong with watching the slaves dance," she said, trying to reassure herself even more than Peachy.

"Of course there's nothing wrong . . . if we don't get caught!" Again Peachy giggled.

The worshipers began leaving the churchyard. Ann realized it was time to return home and get ready for the afternoon meal.

She worked with Myrtilla in putting up the drop-leafed dining table and arranging four chairs around it. Then, under her mother's direction, Ann set the table, making sure that every piece of cutlery was in its proper place.

After dinner, at her mother's request, Ann recited parts of the church's catechism, which she had begun to memorize from the time she was six. She worked on her sampler, but she was so nervous and fidgety that most of the stitches had to be pulled out and done over. She tried entertaining her baby brother by rolling a ball to him, but the ball smacked against the leg of a small table, sending a creamware plate to the floor.

Ann picked up the broken halves of the plate. "I'm sorry, Mama," she said.

"It was an accident," Mrs. McKenzie said, but her face showed her concern. She pressed a hand against Ann's forehead. "You haven't been yourself all day, Ann. Are you ill?"

"No, Mama," Ann said.

"You aren't feverish," her mother answered. She suddenly looked hopeful. "Why don't you find something instructive and pleasurable to do?"

Mulier cum sola cogitat male cogitat, Ann thought. Matthew had told her that this Latin phrase meant "Make the best of everything."

She smiled as she realized she had learned many Latin phrases. Now might be a very good time to surprise her father with her knowledge of Latin. He was in his study, reading, but he'd make time for her.

As she entered the room, her father looked up and smiled. He put down his book, as she'd known he would.

"Papa," Ann said as she perched on the small chair next to his desk, *"asinus asino, et sus sui pulcher."*

His mouth opened in astonishment. "What did you say?"

Gleefully Ann repeated the Latin phrase. "I'm learning Latin, Papa. Matthew is teaching me words and phrases, which I memorize. I just said, 'I wish you a good afternoon.'"

Dr. McKenzie's mouth twitched. "I'm afraid that's not what you said, Ann. The phrase you spoke can be translated into the English language as 'A donkey is beautiful to a donkey, and a pig to a pig.'"

"What?" Ann clapped her hands to her cheeks. "But

Matthew told me . . ." She stopped, her face burning with both anger and embarrassment.

Dr. McKenzie asked, "What else did Matthew teach you?"

Eyes downcast, Ann said, "*Prima caritas incipit a se ipso.* Matthew told me it means 'Thank you very much.'"

"That's not correct, Ann. It means 'Charity begins first with oneself.'"

"What about '*Mulier cum sola cogitat male cogitat*'? Matthew told me it means 'Make the best of everything.'"

Dr. McKenzie's lips twitched again. "That phrase can best be translated as 'When a woman is alone with her thoughts, she is plotting mischief.'"

Ann swallowed hard. Her throat hurt, and her face burned. "Papa," she managed to say, "each time, before Matthew begins our Latin lesson, he waits for me to say, '*Maiori cedo.*' He told me that this means 'I am ready for my lesson.' Was he telling me the truth?"

"I'm afraid not, Ann," Dr. McKenzie answered. "The best translation for '*Maiori cedo*' would be 'I yield to a superior.'"

"A superior!" Ann exclaimed. "Do you mean that over and over I told Matthew that he was my superior?"

"Apparently so." Even though he seemed to be trying hard to suppress it, laughter bubbled up from Dr.

McKenzie's throat. As Ann waited quietly, her fury at Matthew growing by the second, Dr. McKenzie drew a handkerchief from his pocket and wiped his eyes.

Finally he was able to speak. "Can you tell me how it happened that Matthew taught you these phrases?" he asked.

Ann leaned forward. "Who else would teach me Latin, Papa? Not even you. Matthew said he would teach me if I solved his mathematics problems for him, and—"

Dr. McKenzie took her hands in his. "Begin at the beginning, daughter. Tell me about this arrangement."

Ann took a deep breath and told her father everything that had happened.

"Has Matthew learned how to do the problems his tutor assigned him?"

"I don't know," Ann said.

"So the money his father has spent for a tutor has gone to waste."

"Oh," Ann said. "I didn't think of that. Matthew said it would just be a fine trick to play on his tutor."

"Do you know his tutor?"

"Yes, Papa. His name is George Dunn."

"I know young Mr. Dunn. He's a hardworking student at the college. The money he earns as a tutor helps to pay his living and college expenses."

A lump of misery pressed against Ann's chest. "I didn't think of that," she whispered.

"What will people think of Mr. Dunn's teaching ability if Matthew doesn't learn mathematics?"

A tear rolled down Ann's cheek, but she didn't try to rub it away. "I'm so sorry, Papa," she said. "What am I going to do?"

"Suppose you answer that question yourself," he said.

Ann sniffed and gulped. "I'll apologize to Mr. Dunn," she said. "And to Mr. Davenport." She raised her head, worried by a new idea. "But if I do, Mr. Dunn will still be in trouble because Mr. Davenport will think he can't control his student."

"Then what's your answer?" Dr. McKenzie asked quietly.

"I'll stop doing Matthew's problems. Instead, I'll teach him how to do them."

"Very good. That is a fine plan. Tell him today."

She thought about the gathering that would take place within a few hours. She didn't want anything to spoil that adventure. "I'll tell him tomorrow," she said. "I'll also tell him that if he doesn't try to learn, then I'll inform his father and Mr. Dunn what we did, and he'll be in terrible trouble."

Dr. McKenzie leaned back in his chair. "Teaching Matthew will be enough. Threatening him will not be necessary."

"Yes, Papa," Ann said. But she thought, *He doesn't know Matthew.*

Dr. McKenzie beamed at Ann, and she could see the love in his eyes. "Daughter," he said, "since you are so eager to learn Latin, *I* will become your Latin teacher. Your mother may have a few objections at first—" He broke off with a chuckle, then continued. "But I'll reason with her. There's really no harm in your gaining a little knowledge of a classical language."

Ann jumped up. She leaned over and kissed her father's cheek. "Thank you, Papa," she said. She was pleased with his offer to teach her, but she still felt a bit sad. He had made his promise out of love, not because he took seriously her ambition to become a doctor.

As she walked toward the dining room to help set up the table again for an eight o'clock supper, Ann frowned at the job she'd have in teaching mean, horrid old Matthew the mathematics he should have learned from Mr. Dunn. Yet this was the only way to keep him—and herself, too—from getting into even more serious trouble.

"Matthew, you will pay the piper for what you did," she muttered under her breath. "Just wait. I'll think of something."

Chapter Ten

Ann found it hard to eat. She felt as if a ball were bouncing inside her stomach, and her throat was tight and scratchy. Over and over she reminded herself that there was nothing wrong in going to watch the dancers, and nothing wrong in not telling her parents she was going. After all, never once had either of them said, "If you want to watch the slaves dance, you must ask permission." Never!

Eager for bedtime to arrive, Ann tucked away her knitting by the time the clock in the hallway had finished striking nine.

"Good night, Mama. Good night, Papa," she said, and raced up the stairs to bed.

She took off her clothes, except for her stays, which she'd never be able to lace by herself, and laid them on the chair. Hoping that her mother wouldn't notice the absence of the stays, Ann climbed under the quilt, tucking it around her ears. She waited for her mother to tap lightly at her door and give her a good-night kiss.

It seemed almost forever before her mother's cool lips touched her forehead. "Sleep well, daughter," Mrs. McKenzie said.

As she heard the door of her parents' room close, Ann dressed, then lumped the bolster under her quilt to make it look as if she were there, sleeping. She tucked her hair into her cap and quietly, holding her breath, slipped down the stairs and out the back door.

When she reached the apothecary, Peachy, John, and Matthew greeted her in whispers. Ann would have liked to shout at Matthew that she had discovered his mean trickery, but she couldn't. She had to hold her tongue or she'd spoil this evening for all of them.

Walking to the dance site, Matthew and John reminded Ann of a pair of pigeons. Chests out, heads held high, they strutted ahead of Peachy and Ann, who followed them quietly down the dark streets.

As they reached the road that led to Waller's Grove, John Geddy nodded to Ann. "Don't worry. We'll protect you," he said.

Protect us from what? Ann wondered.

Peachy leaned close to whisper, "I'm nervous. Are you?"

"Nervous about what?" Ann whispered back.

"What if a slave patrol comes?"

"Don't be silly," Ann told Peachy. "They won't. It will be a celebration. It will just be a group of people sharing a good time."

Ann forgot what her parents might say about what she was doing. She began to feel much better. She stood up straighter and smiled at Peachy. "This will be fun."

They skirted the groups of slaves who were arriving and found a place behind some trees next to the clearing.

In the center of the clearing, a bonfire blazed. On a log a few feet away from the bonfire sat a man holding two sticks and a large, hollowed-out log. Over the top of the log some kind of smooth animal skin was tightly stretched to make a drum.

Next to the drummer sat a man with a strange musical instrument resting on his legs. It looked like a gourd with a hole cut into the wide part. A large skin was stretched over the hole. A piece of wood with pegs in it came out of one end of the gourd. Ann could see what seemed to be three taut strings or wires stretched across the hole in the gourd all the way to the top end of the neck. "What is that?" she asked the boys.

"It's a *banjar*," Matthew answered. He looked smug.

"A *banjar*," John repeated. He tried to look as all-knowing as Matthew.

"It's a kind of musical instrument," Matthew added.

"That's right," John said.

Ann's curiosity was stronger than her anger at Matthew. "What does a *banjar* do?"

"Listen when they begin to play," Matthew said self-importantly. "You'll see."

The clearing was filling up. Ann saw Cato and Old Betty. Then Myrtilla arrived with Silver. Ann looked for Mrs. Blaikley's slaves, but none of them had come.

Suddenly the music started. The drummer pounded out a rhythm on his drum, and the man with the *banjar* plucked the strings.

Many of the people began to sway with the music, clapping their hands. A few slapped out the rhythm on their thighs. A group of women pulled out white kerchiefs and gracefully waved them over their heads as they danced. One woman began to sing, and others quickly joined in. As the pace of the music quickened, two boys, no older than Ann, hopped and jumped. Ann gasped as one of them leapt over the bonfire.

Before long, Ann found herself swaying to the music, too. She had never heard anything like it. It was fast and unfamiliar, but so joyful she couldn't hold still. She began to clap in rhythm.

Peachy tugged at Ann's skirt. "Ann!" she whispered, and Ann sheepishly stopped clapping.

Ann carefully listened to the words of the songs, but

she couldn't understand them. "What are they saying?" she asked John.

"I don't know," John answered.

But Matthew leaned against a tree and grinned knowingly. "It's probably a language from Africa. A few of the slaves around here were brought from there."

For the first time it occurred to Ann that some of the slaves had a different homeland, a place where they had been born and had lived as children.

Williamsburg was her homeland. She couldn't imagine leaving it. But if she had to, she knew her family would be with her. Ann felt a sudden chill as she wondered what it would be like to be taken away from her family and home, knowing she'd never be able to go back.

Peachy stood and spoke into Ann's ear. "We don't belong here. Let's go home!"

The music swelled into a faster-paced dance that made Ann's feet begin to tap.

In front of her a group of women suddenly stepped out to the rhythm. Ann felt the music ripple through her body. She dashed forward, squeezing in between Old Betty and a young woman. Laughing, she whirled so fast she lost her balance and sat down hard on the ground.

The dancing stopped, and the music and laughter died out. Everyone stared at Ann. Some of the men and women smiled, but most of them frowned. Others looked suspiciously toward the edge of the clearing, where Matthew, Peachy, and John now stood.

Ann felt her face grow hot with embarrassment. "I'm—I'm sorry," she stammered as she struggled to her feet. "The music was so exciting. I just wanted to . . ."

Old Betty tried to brush off Ann's skirt. "Oh, oh," she said. "Mud's all over that pretty gown."

She wrapped an arm around Ann's shoulder as a voice from the crowd asked, "What are you children doing here?"

Myrtilla stepped forward. "You can trust these children," she said. "They won't tell the slave patrol we're here."

"What if they tell their parents?" asked another voice.

"They won't tell anyone," Myrtilla promised.

"I think we should leave," a woman suggested.

Ann began to apologize again, but John and Peachy hurried forward. John firmly gripped Ann's right arm, and Peachy clutched her left. Together they pulled Ann away from the dancers. They tugged her around the outskirts of the crowd and out to the roadway.

"What were you doing?" Peachy demanded.

"We came only to watch the slaves," John scolded, "not dance with them."

Matthew ambled up behind them, grinning. "I enjoyed seeing Ann's performance," he said.

Ann felt herself blushing again. "I liked their music," she said. "I . . . I felt like joining in."

Matthew shook his head sadly, but his grin didn't fade. "My, my. What would your mother say if she had seen you?"

Ann gasped. "You won't tell her?"

"I didn't say I would."

Ann sighed with relief, but Matthew continued, "But then, I didn't say I wouldn't."

Peachy jabbed her brother on the shoulder. "Matthew, behave yourself. You won't tell, because you'd be in trouble, too. You're the one who thought of this idea."

Matthew scowled at his sister. "Who says so?"

"I say so," Peachy answered. "And I'll be glad to say so to everybody and anybody who will listen."

Matthew shrugged. "Truce," he said. "None of us will ever again speak about this evening."

"Agreed," John said.

Ann and Peachy nodded.

"However, there are memories here I'll never forget," Matthew said. His grin returned.

"Is that so?" Ann snapped. "Well, never forget this, either: *Mulier cum sola cogitat male cogitat.*"

For an instant Matthew looked puzzled. Then he

grinned at Ann and said, "Oh, yes. 'Make the best of everything.'"

Ann didn't answer. She just smiled. Matthew didn't know how wrong he was. But he'd soon find out that a woman alone with her thoughts could plot some really fine mischief—against him!

Chapter Eleven

On a bright morning two days later, Ann didn't bounce out of bed as she usually did. Her stomach hurt, and the idea of eating breakfast made her feel even worse. When Mrs. McKenzie laced Ann's stays, Ann let out a groan. "Too tight!" she cried out.

Her mother's eyebrows rose in surprise. "The laces are no tighter than usual."

"Yes, they are, Mama. My stomach hurts."

Mrs. McKenzie felt Ann's forehead and said, "No fever, thank goodness." For a few moments she studied Ann. "You're probably just hungry. You ate very little at supper last night."

"I'm not hungry now," Ann said.

Before Ann could stop her, Mrs. McKenzie picked up a petticoat Ann had left on the chair and opened the clothes press.

"I'll take care of that, Mama," Ann cried.

"What's this?" Mrs. McKenzie bent to pick up the gown Ann had worn to the gathering and had wadded in the bottom of the press. She held up the gown and immediately saw the streaks of dried mud on the back of the skirt. Puzzled, she asked, "Ann, how in the world did your gown get muddy?"

Ann's stomach gave a lurch. She had hoped to add the gown to the dirty clothes on the next washday without her mother's discovering it. Now what would she do? "I—um—slipped and fell," she said.

"When? On Sunday you wore this gown until evening, when you went upstairs to bed. You haven't worn it since, so how—?" Mrs. McKenzie frowned sternly at Ann. "I believe you may have something to tell me, Ann. I am ready to hear it."

Ann took a deep breath. She backed up to the bed and sat, her legs refusing to hold her up. "I went out at nine o'clock Sunday night with Peachy, John, and Matthew."

Mrs. McKenzie gave a shocked gasp. "You left the house at night without permission? Pray tell me why. What in the world did you children do?"

Ann's voice felt small and far away. "We wanted to watch the dancing at the slave gathering."

Mrs. McKenzie dropped to the bed beside Ann. "Oh, Ann! I can't believe you'd do this," she said. "I thought I had taught you to respect your position in life. You must remember that your lessons included the proper way to conduct yourself with slaves." Her voice rose in anger. "How could you have risked sullying your good name— and ours—by ignoring everything you've learned?"

"I'm sorry, Mama," Ann murmured.

Mrs. McKenzie clutched the bedpost to steady herself as she slowly got to her feet. "I will discuss this with your father," she said. "While I'm occupied, you take care of William. Keep him busy. He's old enough to get into everything."

"Yes, Mama," Ann answered meekly. Her mother was angry enough; Ann dreaded what her father would say. Why had she gone to the gathering? She'd known better. Had she done so just because Matthew had taunted her and said she couldn't? Ann groaned and held one hand to her aching forehead. At the moment she didn't know what she'd been thinking.

She walked downstairs to the kitchen, where William was playing. She took his hand and led him into the parlor.

"Bear," William said. He crawled around a chair, growling.

Ann knew what was expected of her. She had taught the game to William. Playing bear would keep him busy, and it would keep her mind from the scolding she would soon get.

"I'm a bear, too," she said to William, trying to get into the spirit of the game. "I'm a big bear who's going to catch the little bear." She got to her knees and growled, sending the little bear squealing and scrambling away as fast as he could.

But Ann stopped and groaned again. Crawling on the floor made her stomach feel even worse. "Come with me, baby bear," she said to William. "I'll read a book to you."

Ann took down a child's hornbook from a shelf in her father's study. She gazed at it a moment, then shook her head and put it back. It wouldn't hold William's interest. He was so young that he needed drawings to look at. Ann reached for another book. It was a medical book, illustrated with sketches of parts of the human body. The book had fascinated her when she was a small child and still did.

As William climbed into Ann's lap, she opened the book to a page with an illustration. "Here's a foot," she said to William. "Let's count the toes. One . . . two . . . three . . ."

Ann's head began to ache. Much as she loved playing with William, she was relieved when their mother picked him up and announced that breakfast was ready.

"Where's Papa?" Ann asked in surprise.

Mrs. McKenzie tucked William into a chair, then seated herself. "Your father was called early this morning to Mrs. Blaikley's home," she said. She frowned at Ann as she added, "We'll discuss your behavior when he returns."

Ann chose not to think about her mother's last remark. But she was alarmed when her mother mentioned Mrs. Blaikley.

Just then the door opened and Dr. McKenzie strode into the room.

"Papa, how is Mrs. Blaikley?" Ann cried out.

"She has smallpox," he answered. He took his place at the table and spread his napkin across his lap.

Myrtilla put a bowl of hominy in front of him, but he just poked at it with his spoon. "Three of the Blaikley slaves also have the smallpox, and I expect the fourth will be ill with it soon."

"Lucy," Ann whispered.

Dr. McKenzie gave Ann a puzzled glance. "Yes. Lucy is one of the slaves who is ill."

Mrs. McKenzie looked frightened. "The disease seems to be spreading rapidly. The Dawsons, the Holloways, and now Katherine Blaikley."

"And one of the Geddys' slaves—Old Betty. I believe we are in for a more severe epidemic of smallpox than we had feared," Dr. McKenzie said.

Ann leaned back in her chair. "Papa," she said in a small voice, "how do you know if someone is ill with smallpox? Is it because you see pox on their bodies?"

Dr. McKenzie shook his head. "The pox don't show for at least five days," he said. "At first the person who is ill suffers nausea and severe headaches. As a rule, small-pox victims run fevers, which can be dangerous, and there is often pain in the back and in the muscles."

"What about the pox?"

"Red spots don't appear until the third day. Then they spread from the face, neck, and arms to the rest of the body. By the fifth or sixth day, they develop into the large blisters we call pox. These blisters dry into crusts. The crusts finally drop off in three to four weeks."

"Such a long time!" Mrs. McKenzie said.

"That it is, and the patient remains infectious from the beginning of the disease until the last crust disappears."

"Kenneth, there is something else we need to discuss," Mrs. McKenzie said. She quickly told him about Ann's escapade two nights before.

Ann often saw indulgent humor in her father's eyes when her mother reported Ann's misbehavior, but this time she saw anger, and she shrank back in her chair.

"That was unthinkable, daughter!" Dr. McKenzie exclaimed. "Sneaking out of the house is completely unacceptable. And willfully attending an illegal event is atrocious behavior."

"I—I'm sorry, Papa," Ann stammered, but Dr. McKenzie ignored her apology.

He had a great deal more to say about Ann's transgression, but finally he leaned toward her, his anger spent, and Ann could see the worry and fear in his eyes.

"Don't you realize," he said, "that you also endangered your life? With smallpox spreading, I have tried to keep you, your mother, and William away from crowds as much as possible except for attending church services. From what your mother told me, you were in contact with Old Betty, who is now ill with the pox."

Ann closed her eyes, wishing that the horrible pain in her head would disappear. "Worse than that, Papa, I was with Mrs. Blaikley's slave, Lucy, last week," she murmured.

As Ann's headache deepened, the room whirled around her, and voices came from so far away that she couldn't tell what they said. She felt herself sliding out of her chair. "Oh, Papa, help me," she murmured before she slipped into darkness.

Ann became lost in fever dreams. She burned. She ached. Spoonfuls of strange-tasting medicine oozed between her lips and trickled down her throat. She heard her father say, "For the fever," and her mother answer, "And cool water. I am bathing her with wet cloths as often as possible."

The cool, damp cloths against her forehead, neck,

back, and chest sometimes made Ann shiver. But after her mother's treatment the fever always abated, and she slid into peaceful dreams, rocking in a comfortable sea until the fever roared back.

"Keep your fingers away from the pustules," her father said more than once, and Ann tried to obey. But she was more aware of her mother, who seemed to be constantly at her side, cooling her face, helping her to sip spoonfuls of spearmint tea for the nausea, and holding her hand to comfort her.

Finally, one morning, Ann awoke to find her bedding and shift wet with perspiration but her body cool. The fever had broken, and Ann knew that she was past the worst of the disease and would recover.

The sky was already bright with the promise of a hot, sunny day. Where was her mother at this late hour?

Ann climbed from bed, so wobbly that she had to cling to the bedpost to stay on her feet. But step by step she walked to the looking glass that rested on her dressing table and leaned to peer into it.

The pustules on her face were horrible, ugly blots. She grimaced as she realized each would leave a scar. She could only be grateful that there weren't too many of them.

"Mama?" Ann called.

But her mother didn't answer.

Feeble from the days in bed, Ann slowly made her

way to her parents' bedchamber. She knocked at the door.

When no one answered, she knocked again. This time she heard a faint moan.

Ann opened the door and saw that both her parents were in bed and William was in his cradle. From the deep red flush and spots on their faces, she knew that all three were ill with the pox.

"I'll take care of you," Ann promised. "And I'll get Myrtilla to help."

Ann wobbled back to her room, where she pulled off her damp clothing. Using the water that remained in the bowl on her bedside table, she washed herself quickly. As fast as possible, she put on a clean shift, a petticoat, a loose short gown, stockings, and shoes. With trembling hands, she clung to the banister and managed to climb down the stairs. Shakily she walked out the back door to the small building where Myrtilla and Silver slept.

Myrtilla answered Ann's knock. With pustules all over her face, she looked as ill as Ann had been.

"Do you still have fever?" Ann asked.

"No," Myrtilla answered. "Fever's gone. So has Silver's."

"If you're able, I need your help," Ann said. "Mama, Papa, and William are all ill."

Myrtilla took a long breath. "I can help some, child.

But maybe you should send for relatives or friends to lend a hand."

"There's no one to ask," Ann said. "No one who hasn't had the disease should come into a house with smallpox." She stood a little straighter. She desperately wanted to collapse into bed, but she was the only one who could help. "If you're able," she said again to Myrtilla, "will you make a pot of tea?"

"I'm able, Mistress Ann," Myrtilla answered.

So Ann hurried upstairs with spoons, a bucket of cool water, and clean cloths. A bottle of a dark liquid rested on the table near her father. Ann sniffed it. It was the medicine he had given to her for the fever. She poured a spoonful and fed it to her father, opening his lips and making sure the liquid ran down his throat and not out of his mouth. She fed the same medicine to her mother. Hoping she was doing the right thing, she gave half a spoonful to William.

She washed her father's and mother's faces with cool water, then picked up her little brother, holding him on her lap. Heat poured in waves from his body, so she took off his shift and dampened him all over with a wet, cool cloth.

When he stopped fretting and relaxed against her, she covered his bare bottom with a fresh, folded clout and slipped a clean shift over his head.

As Myrtilla spoon-fed tea to Dr. and Mrs. McKenzie,

Ann held William, rocking him in her arms and singing lullabies. As he drifted off into a comfortable sleep, Ann lowered him into his cradle.

Myrtilla leaned over William. "That poor, poor baby," she murmured.

"It's important that he take something more than a few spoonfuls of tea," Ann said. "He needs milk. I'll tempt him by adding a little sugar to it."

Myrtilla looked concerned. "He's used to his mama feedin' him."

"He's almost two. Mama would soon be weaning him in any case. Besides, William loves pudding and sweet things. I think he'll like the sweetened milk. Do you think you can get any milk for him?"

Myrtilla nodded. "I'll see that some's brought by. Want me to make some barley soup, too?"

At the mention of barley soup, Ann's stomach growled loudly.

"You're gettin' well, child," Myrtilla said, and they both laughed.

"The soup will be good for you and for Silver, too," Ann said. "Make sure there is plenty. And then rest, Myrtilla. See that Silver rests, too. Some of the household tasks can wait. It's important that you not become overtired."

As soon as the soup was made, Ann fed her mother

a few spoonfuls. Mrs. McKenzie finally gave a contented sigh, closed her eyes, and went back to sleep.

But Dr. McKenzie swallowed only two spoonfuls of the soup before he turned his head away. Weakly he tried to get out of bed. "I must tend to my patients," he murmured.

"First let me tend to you," Ann said. She eased him back, tucked the quilt around him, and smoothed his pillow. "Once you are well, then you can care for others who are ill."

He looked up into Ann's face and asked, "William? How does he?"

"Very well, Papa," Ann said. "I keep him comfortable, and he was able to hold down the sugared milk I fed him. Now, open your mouth so that I may feed you more soup."

"The medicine for the fever . . ."

"I am using it for both you and Mama. I'm giving William a smaller dose, and it seems to help."

For a moment Dr. McKenzie was silent. Then he said, "You are a good doctor, Ann."

Delighted with his praise, Ann impulsively reached out to hug him. But she stopped herself in time and said, "Thank you, Papa. Now you must obey your doctor's instructions. Open your mouth. You need more soup."

Dr. McKenzie did as she told him. Ann fed him, then waited until he fell asleep.

It was much later before Ann could sit still long enough to enjoy her own bowl of soup. There was bedding to change and chamber pots to empty. Ann remembered her mother's good care, and she tried to do everything her mother had done. She pressed wet cloths to her parents' hot faces and bathed William's feverish body. She checked Silver to make sure he had no traces of fever and was as clean and comfortable as possible.

At the end of the week, the McKenzies had an unexpected visitor. Ann was crossing the downstairs passage when someone knocked on the front door so loudly that she started.

She hurried to the door and opened it to see Matthew standing on the front steps.

For a few moments he stared at her, open-mouthed. "I heard you had the pox," he said. "Peachy has it, too. My mother sent me to the apothecary shop to get something for her fever, but no one's there, not even Zachary Twill. The shop is locked. Could Dr. McKenzie—"

"He's ill with the pox, too," Ann said. "Everyone in our household is ill—even the servants. We've had word that Mr. Twill has also taken sick."

Matthew's eyes widened. "Who's caring for you?"

"I am," Ann said. "I'm over the worst of the disease, so I'm caring for the others."

Matthew backed off the steps. "I'll find another apothecary. I'm sorry I bothered you."

"Don't go," Ann said quickly. "I know what medicine Peachy should take. I'll get it for you. Wait for me outside the apothecary. Don't get close to me, though. I'm still contagious."

She closed the front door, ran to get the key to the shop, and hurried to open the apothecary door. She found the bottle of the mixture her father had given her, matching the Latin name on the label to the name on the bottle in the bedchamber. To make very sure, she sniffed the bottle and tasted a drop on her finger. Yes. It was definitely the same mixture. She poured the medicine from the large bottle into a smaller one and took it outside.

Careful to stay a few feet away from Matthew, Ann put the bottle of medicine down on the ground. "Give Peachy one spoonful as her fever rises," she said. "And tell your mother to dampen her face, neck, chest, and arms with cool water. Make sure that Peachy gets enough liquid to drink. If her stomach is still upset, try spearmint tea. It will usually stay down. When she begins to feel better, have some milk puddings made for her. Keep her bedding and her shift changed and dry. If

Peachy is kept comfortable, she'll find it easier to sleep, and plenty of sleep will help her to recover."

Ann stopped, a lump in her throat as she looked at Matthew. "Pray tell Peachy that I miss her and I want her to get well again very, very soon."

As she began to walk toward the house, Matthew seemed to collect his thoughts. In a respectful voice he called out, "I thank you, Ann." He picked up the bottle of medicine and put it into a pocket of his coat. Then he added, "The way you talked to me . . . it was exactly the way a doctor would talk."

Ann shut the door of the house behind her and leaned against it, enjoying Matthew's words over and over in her mind. She smiled and whispered aloud, "I talk like a doctor. I *am* like a doctor. Papa told me I'm a good doctor!"

From upstairs William let out a loud, healthy wail. "Ann-Ann!" he shouted. "Thirsty!"

"I'm coming!" Ann called.

Forgetting to behave like a proper young lady, Ann snatched up her skirts and struggled up the stairs as fast as she could go.

Chapter Twelve

Caring for everyone—even with Myrtilla's help—was an exhausting job, but Ann was rewarded when all her patients began to recover.

The first evening when her parents were able to come downstairs Ann turned into a celebration. She got out the blue-and-white delftware, then served Dr. and Mrs. McKenzie glasses of apple cider and thin, crisp ginger cakes.

Dressed in loose clothes—her father in his Oriental-style banyan and her mother in a short gown—they relaxed in the parlor. They were both thinner and pale, and a few crusts still marked their faces. But they had passed through the worst of the disease and, to Ann's relief, they would soon be strong and well.

Mrs. McKenzie sighed happily. "It's so good to be out of bed," she said. She beamed at Ann. "Your care couldn't have been better. You were a wonderful help to us all."

Ann smiled. "I learned from you, Mama. I did all the things for you that you did for me when I was so ill."

In his cradle upstairs William called out, "Mama? Ann-Ann?"

"He's awake," Ann said. She rose from her chair, but Mrs. McKenzie got to her feet.

"I'll go," she said. "I'm eager to help my little one again."

As Mrs. McKenzie left the parlor, Dr. McKenzie said to Ann, "You were skillful in caring for the household, daughter. I'm very proud of you."

Ann blushed at his praise. She perched on the settee next to him and said, "I was being a doctor, just like you."

Dr. McKenzie shook his head. "No, Ann. Not like me. I tell the patient what disease is making him ill, and I prescribe medications and herbs that might make him more comfortable. But you cared constantly for your patients, through day and night. You helped them to get well, the same as your mother did for you."

"But Mama isn't a doctor," Ann protested. "People who are ill don't send for her."

"She wouldn't want them to. She cares for her family, and she'd gladly go immediately to take care of a relative, a friend, or a neighbor who needed help."

Dr. McKenzie put an arm around Ann's shoulders and held her close. "Dearest daughter," he said, "universities will not allow you to join them to study medicine. People who are ill will never ask for your help as a doctor. No one accepts a woman doctor."

"They accept Mrs. Blaikley."

"Not as a doctor, but as a midwife. She ministers to women and their children."

Ann sighed with disappointment. "Do you mean that women have the sense to accept a woman's help, but men don't?"

Dr. McKenzie chuckled. "You have a good point, Ann. But I have one, too. If you apply to study to become a doctor, you'll become involved in a fight you can't win. Why not try to be as good a wife, mother, and friend as your own mother is? In that way you'll be able to give your family the best of yourself."

Nestling close to her father, Ann thought about what he had said. She still had a few reservations. "There are lots of things about being a wife and mother I don't look forward to doing," she told him. "I hate making tiny stitches in my sewing."

He smiled. "There are distasteful parts in any job. I hate cleaning out rotten, smelly sores."

Ann wondered what the distasteful parts of a midwife's job were. She would ask Mrs. Blaikley and hope for an answer. Someday she might become a midwife, so she'd need to know. She remembered the joy on Mrs. Fox's face as she held her new baby, and the grumpy, sour expression on Mr. Davis's face as he complained about what Dr. McKenzie had told him to do to get well. It seemed that a midwife would have much nicer patients than a doctor would. That was certainly something to give thought to.

Myrtilla came into the room. As she handed two envelopes to Dr. McKenzie, she said quietly, "Silver was out this mornin' and heard the news from the Geddy house."

Ann sat up straight. "The Geddys have the pox, too?"

"Yes, Mistress Ann," Myrtilla answered. "The whole household came down with it."

"Do they need help?"

"Not now. They're most over it and gettin' well. 'Cept for Cato and Old Betty." Myrtilla bowed her head, a mournful look on her face.

Fearful of what she was going to hear, Ann gripped the arm of the settee and held her breath.

"Did Cato and Old Betty die of the disease?" Dr. McKenzie asked.

Myrtilla could only nod. She turned and left the room.

"They died!" Ann wailed.

Dr. McKenzie looked puzzled. "Smallpox is a serious

disease. Some people do die from it. Surely you knew that."

"Yes, I knew, but I didn't think about it. When you and Mama and William were so ill, I *couldn't* think about anyone dying. I was frightened enough." She burst into tears. "Oh, Papa!" she cried. "Old Betty dying . . . Cato dying . . . She leaned against her father and cried until there were no more tears. He didn't speak. He just held her and waited until she was ready to talk.

Finally Ann raised her head. "The night of the slaves' gathering I was coming down with smallpox and didn't know it. I gave Old Betty the disease. I killed her!" A few leftover tears rolled down Ann's cheeks. "You were right. I know I shouldn't have gone. I wanted to be at the gathering because Matthew was going. He laughed at me and said girls couldn't go. So I told him they could."

Dr. McKenzie sighed. "You weren't responsible for the deaths of Cato and Old Betty," he said. "The entire town of Williamsburg is suffering an epidemic of smallpox. The Geddy slaves probably came into contact with the disease through many sources."

Ann sighed with relief. "It's not my fault? Really? Oh, Papa, I felt so guilty."

"I didn't say you were without guilt," he told her,

"but your guilt does not come from spreading small-pox; you are guilty of leaving the house at night without permission and attending the slaves' gathering. Remember, you and your friends ought not to treat our slaves as equals. You should have respected our instructions about how to behave toward slaves—be kind but never forget your place and theirs."

"I'm truly sorry, Papa," Ann said.

"I'll accept your apology, daughter, if I have your assurance that behavior like this will not happen again."

Ann nodded. "I'll not sneak out of the house ever again. I promise."

"Very well. I trust you to keep your promise."

Ann leaned against her father and was silent for a few moments. She thought about the music and the dancing and how the music had filled her body and she'd had to answer it. She smiled. "It was a wonderful gathering, Papa, with a drum and a *banjar*. The bonfire crackled and sparks flew out, and there was singing and laughing. It was much more fun than the Christmas ball you and Mama gave."

Dr. McKenzie raised one eyebrow. "I'm afraid you're not feeling quite as guilty as you should. I think we'll speak further about this matter on a later occasion, when your mother can join us."

Sighing, Ann could only nod. Her mother would

have plenty to say. It would be an unhappy lesson, but Ann knew she would deserve it.

She was surprised when her father said, "These letters Myrtilla brought are addressed to you. Would you like to open them?"

Ann pulled away, sat upright, and reached for the envelopes. "They're for me?"

As she tore open the first envelope she said, "Oh! Good! This one's from Peachy!" Ann read the first part of the note quickly, then smiled at her father. "Peachy wrote that most of her family are over the worst of the pox—except for Matthew, who isn't nearly as ill as the rest of them had been but who is carrying on like a baby. He's sure he's not getting enough attention and is afraid he will die. Then Peachy says she's bored and hopes I can come to visit soon for more games of whist."

As she turned the page over and read the rest of Peachy's message, Ann yelped with delight. "Papa! Listen to this! Peachy's father said that with all the burgesses worried about coming down with smallpox, they don't know when they'll be able to hold a meeting, so nothing will be done for a time about a vote to move the capital away from Williamsburg. He has heard that the general feeling is that we should keep the capital here. Since most of the citizens will have already had the smallpox and become immune to the disease, it will be the safest place in the colony in which to meet."

"That *is* good news," Dr. McKenzie said. "I have no wish to move my house and apothecary."

Wiggling with happiness, Ann opened the second envelope. "This one is from Matthew," she said. She read the note and laughed. "It seems that with all the others in the family needing their mother's attention, Matthew doesn't think he is getting enough good care. Listen to this, Papa. 'Ann, you seem to know how to doctor and have cared well for your own family and household (which I heard from my mother's personal slave). So I call upon you, as a good friend, to come to my aid by spending some time taking care of me. I especially like milk puddings and spearmint tea.'"

Ann laughed so hard she bent over, holding her stomach. Finally she sat up, an exciting plan beginning to grow in her mind.

"Papa," she said, "the last few crusts on my pox have gone, so I'm no longer contagious to people on the street. May I leave the house and visit the Davenports this evening?"

"I think that would be a kind and thoughtful gesture," Dr. McKenzie said. "But be sure to ask your mother's permission, too."

"Yes, Papa," Ann said. Her mother was always willing to help a neighbor in need. She'd be glad to allow Ann to help care for Matthew.

Ann remembered that in a chest upstairs lay a length

of white cotton fabric. It was long enough to wrap over and around her and around the top of the skull her father kept on his bookcase. If she held the skull on her head and glided into Matthew's room at dusk . . .

She grinned. *Now it's time for you to pay the piper, Matthew,* she thought. She could picture Matthew screaming in fright and leaping from his bed. His brothers and sisters would come running. They'd laugh at Matthew, too. They'd all laugh, and—

Dr. McKenzie interrupted Ann's thoughts. "In spite of impetuous ways that sometimes lead you into trouble, you're a good girl, Ann," he told her.

Ann smiled. Why should she stoop to Matthew's level? She should forget about playing his kind of silly tricks. Instead, she'd bring him a custard, brew him some tea, and pretend she was a doctor.

Ann eagerly looked forward to the coming visit with the Davenports.

Epilogue

As Molly Otts finished her story, Keisha giggled. "In a way I wish Ann *had* used the skull to pay back Matthew. I wish I could have seen his face."

"Hey! Don't get down on Matthew," Chip said. "I thought he was a pretty cool guy."

"You would. You're a lot like him!" Keisha said.

Chip and Stewart laughed, but Lori sighed.

"Ann wanted to be a doctor when she grew up. I do, too. I hated how everyone tried to discourage her."

Stewart grinned. "Matthew said girls have weaker brains. He was right."

Mrs. Otts smiled as she shook her head. "'Twas once thought that men were superior to women, but women and girls have proved that idea wrong."

"That silly idea is one reason that women weren't allowed to vote, isn't it?" Lori said.

"Women couldn't vote until 1920!" Keisha said. "It took men that long to recognize what was what."

Lori had a sudden thought. "Mrs. Otts, do you know what happened when Ann grew up? Even though she couldn't have been a doctor, she was interested in Mrs. Blaikley's work. Did Ann become a midwife?"

"No," Mrs. Otts answered. "Women who worked at jobs like midwifery were usually widows. Without a husband to care for her and a child to feed, I'm sure Mrs. Blaikley found that job the best way to carry on her life. As for Ann McKenzie, she married at the age of thirty-three. She married a doctor, Dr. David Black of Petersburg. Ann had a son and, to be sure, she must have been a loving, caring wife and mother."

"I bet she knew how to doctor her husband and child when they were sick," Lori said.

"I'm sure she did. She was also responsible for tending to the family slaves when they were ill. But sometimes the slaves chose doctoring ways of their own, brought from their own country," Mrs. Otts said.

"I want to know more about Silver and the other children who were slaves in Williamsburg. Do you know any stories about them?" asked Keisha.

"The lives of slave children in the Williamsburg area were far different in many ways from the lives of the middling sort, like Ann and Peachy and John and Matthew. Until the age of six, children were children,

117

but after that age was reached, young slaves who were growing up lived a hard life."

Mrs. Otts smiled. "I have in mind a fine young man called Caesar, who spent every one of his first nine years as a slave at Carter's Grove plantation. In 1759, when his life took an abrupt turn, he was most unhappy. But slaves had no choice about the direction their futures would take, and Caesar, no matter that his wishes couldn't be granted . . ."

Mrs. Otts stopped speaking and glanced toward the street.

Lori said, "Go on, Mrs. Otts. What did Caesar wish for?"

"Ah, now," Mrs. Otts said as she began to straighten a pile of ribbon-trimmed caps. "I'm sorry to end our visit so abruptly, but here come a goodly number of customers. I can see they will keep me busy. Come back this afternoon, dearies, and I'll be glad to tell you Caesar's story."

Author's Note

The children in Ann McKenzie's story were real people who lived in Williamsburg Virginia, in 1746/47. Until 1752, January, February, and most of March of each year carried the date of the previous year, so when we refer to those months, we give the year a double date.

We know when some of the children of Williamsburg were born and when they died. We have found the dates when some of them married and the names of their children. But old records aren't complete enough to give us a full picture of their individual lives.

From the facts we have about the children's families, from our knowledge of what life in Williamsburg was like during the colonial years, and from the history of the Virginia colony's political situation, we can piece together imaginary situations for the children. This is where the stories begin.

I began researching this book by reading as much as I could about the colonial capital of Virginia, from the founding of the town to the Revolutionary War. I read the history of the colonies and learned about the clothing, the food, the social customs, and the practice of medicine in Williamsburg in 1747. I visited Colonial Williamsburg to do firsthand research, even attending programs with students who had come on field trips.

When it came time to write Ann McKenzie's story, I was fortunate to have help from the historians of The Colonial Williamsburg Foundation. They told me the names of some of the children Ann would most logically have had for friends, and I read the biographies and the genealogies the Foundation has developed for the children's families.

I visited the houses in Colonial Williamsburg's Historic Area where Ann and her friends once lived. It was exciting to imagine Ann helping to set the table for dinner or picking flowers in her garden, or climbing into her post bed at night. I took notes and photographs to help me remember all the small details of the way the rooms were arranged.

I had to imagine what Ann, Peachy, John, and Matthew must have been like when they were children. I put myself in Ann's place and asked, "What if . . . ?"

What if I greatly admired the work my father did as a doctor and desperately longed to be a doctor, too—

even though no one would allow a woman to practice medicine?

What if I enjoyed helping in my father's apothecary, delighting in the ever-present spicy, medicinal, and herbal odors?

What if I were bright and fun-loving and excited about life—always eager to learn new things, to take dares, and to jump into adventures?

I put myself in Ann's place and began to plot the story. The character of Ann grew and developed in my mind, and with her came the characters of Peachy, John, and Matthew.

I'm glad to share with you what we know about the children in this book:

Ann McKenzie was baptized in Williamsburg in 1739. Her father came to the colonies from Scotland.

Would this mean that Ann had reddish gold hair, a scattering of freckles, and the same desire for opportunity that brought her father to Virginia? I think so.

Ann McKenzie could not become a doctor, but when she was thirty-three, in 1772, she married a doctor, Dr. David Black of Petersburg, Virginia. We know that Ann gave birth to one son and named him David Black Jr. Ann's brother, William, studied at the College of William and Mary, then studied medicine in Petersburg under Dr. Black, and also became a doctor.

Peachy Davenport, born in 1737, didn't marry until

1772, when she wed a Williamsburg printer named Alexander Purdie. Alexander supported the patriot cause, so we believe that Peachy did, too. Peachy, who purchased a great deal of property in Williamsburg, was married and widowed three times and had no children.

Matthew Davenport, who was born in Williamsburg in 1734, the eighth child in the Davenport family, was well educated. We think that he studied both with tutors and at the College of William and Mary. Among other positions he held, Matthew succeeded his father as town clerk and as writing master at the college. Records show only the first name of the woman Matthew married in 1762, Frances, but we know that she and Matthew had two children, Margaret and James.

John Geddy was one of eight children—four boys and four girls. No birth dates are known for the seven older children in the Geddy family, but we can guess that John was close to Ann McKenzie's age. John's father, a gunsmith, died in 1744, before John's baby sister was born. It is believed that David and William were the two oldest boys and that they apprenticed with their father. Mrs. Geddy may have hired Mr. Beadle, an indentured servant who had worked for her husband, to run the foundry after Mr. Geddy died. We think that she apprenticed James and John to Samuel Galt, a silversmith who rented property from her. Later David and William carried on their father's trades as gunsmiths, cutlers, and founders, and James and John both became silversmiths.

Enjoy Ann's story. Then ask yourself: "If I were Ann or Peachy or John or Matthew, living in 1747, what would I have done with my life?"

About Williamsburg

The story of Williamsburg, the capital of eighteenth-century Virginia, began more than seventy-five years before the thirteen original colonies became the United States in 1776.

Williamsburg was the colony's second capital. Jamestown, the first permanent English settlement in North America, was the first. Jamestown stood on a swampy peninsula in the James River, and over the years, people found it an unhealthy place to live. They also feared that ships sailing up the river could attack the town.

In 1699, a year after the Statehouse at Jamestown burned down for the fourth time, Virginians decided to move the capital a few miles away, to a place known as Middle Plantation. On high ground between two rivers,

The Capitol in Colonial Williamsburg's Historic Area.

Middle Plantation was a healthier and safer location that was already home to several of Virginia's leading citizens.

Middle Plantation was also the home of the College of William and Mary, today one of Virginia's most revered institutions. The college received its charter from King William III and Queen Mary II of England in 1693. Its graduates include two of our nation's first presidents: Thomas Jefferson and James Monroe.

The new capital's name was changed to Williamsburg in honor of King William. Like the

Virginia colony, Williamsburg grew during the eighteenth century. Government officials and their families arrived. Taverns opened for business, and merchants and artisans settled in. Much of the heavy labor and domestic work was performed by African Americans, most of them slaves, although a few were free. By the eve of the American Revolution, nearly two thousand people—roughly half of them white and half of them black—lived in Williamsburg.

The Revolutionary War and Its Leaders

The formal dates of the American Revolution are 1775 to 1783, but the problems between the thirteen original colonies and Great Britain, their mother country, began in 1765, when Parliament enacted the Stamp Act.

England was in debt from fighting the Seven Years' War (called the French and Indian War in the colonies) and believed that the colonists should help pay the debt. The colonists were stunned. They considered themselves English and believed they had the same political rights as people living in England. These rights included being taxed *only* by an elected body, such as each colony's legislature. Now a body in which they were not represented, Parliament, was taxing them.

All thirteen colonies protested, and the Stamp Act was

repealed in 1766. Over the next eleven years, however, Great Britain imposed other taxes and enacted other laws that the colonists believed infringed on their rights.

A reenactment of Virginia legislators debating the Stamp Act.

Finally, in 1775, the second Continental Congress, made up of representatives from twelve of the colonies, established an army. The following year, the Congress (now with representatives from all thirteen colonies) declared independence from Great Britain.

The Revolutionary War was the historical event that ensured Williamsburg's place in American history. Events that happened there and the people who participated in them helped form the values on which the United States was founded. Virginians meeting in Williamsburg helped lead the thirteen colonies to independence.

In fact, Americans first declared independence in the Capitol building in Williamsburg. There, on May 15, 1776, the colony's leaders declared Virginia's full freedom from England. In a unanimous vote, they also instructed the colony's representatives to the Continental Congress to propose that the Congress "declare the United Colonies free and independent states absolved from all allegiances to or dependence upon the crown or parliament of Great Britain."

Three weeks later, Richard Henry Lee, one of Virginia's delegates, stood before the Congress and proposed independence. His action led directly to the writing of the Declaration of Independence. The Congress adopted the Declaration on July 2 and signed it two days later. The United States of America was born.

Williamsburg served as a training ground for three noteworthy patriots: George Washington, Thomas Jefferson, and Patrick Henry. Each arrived in Williamsburg as a young man, and there each matured into a statesman.

In 1752, George Washington, who later led the American forces to victory over the British in the Revolutionary War and became our nation's first president, came to Williamsburg at the age of nineteen. He soon began a career in the military, which led to a seat in

Virginia's legislature, the House of Burgesses. He served as a burgess for sixteen years—negotiating legislation, engaging in political discussions, and building social and political relationships. These experiences helped mold him into one of America's finest political leaders.

Patrick Henry, who would go on to become the first governor of the Commonwealth of Virginia as well as a powerful advocate for the Bill of Rights, first traveled to Williamsburg in 1760 to obtain a law license. Only twenty-three years old, he barely squeaked through the exam. Five years later, as a first-time burgess, he led Virginia's opposition to the Stamp Act. For the next eleven years, Henry's talent as a speaker—including his now famous Caesar-Brutus speech and the immortal cry, "Give me liberty or give me death!"—rallied Virginians to the patriot cause.

Thomas Jefferson, who later wrote the Declaration of Independence, succeeded Patrick Henry as the governor of Virginia, and became the third president of the United States, arrived in Williamsburg in 1760 at the age of seventeen to attend the College of William and Mary. As the cousin of Peyton Randolph, the respected Speaker of the House of Burgesses, Jefferson was immediately welcomed by Williamsburg society. He became a lawyer and was elected a burgess in 1769. In his very first session, the royal governor closed the legislature because it had protested the Townshend Acts. The burgesses moved the meeting to the Raleigh Tavern, where they drew up an agreement to boycott British goods.

Jefferson, Henry, and Washington each signed the agreement. In the years that followed, all three men supported the patriots' cause and the nation that grew out of it.

Williamsburg Then and Now

Williamsburg in the eighteenth century was a vibrant American town. Thanks largely to the vision of the Reverend Dr. W. A. R. Goodwin, rector of Bruton Parish Church at the opening of the twentieth century, its vitality can still be experienced today. The generosity of philanthropist John D. Rockefeller Jr. made it possible to restore Williamsburg to its eighteenth-century glory. Original colonial buildings were acquired and carefully returned to their eighteenth-century appearance. Later houses and buildings were torn down and replaced by carefully researched reconstructions, most built on original eighteenth-century foundations. Rockefeller gave the project money and enthusiastic support for more than thirty years.

Today, Colonial Williamsburg's Historic Area is a museum and a living city. The restored buildings, antique furnishings, and costumed interpreters can help you create a picture of the past in your mind's eye. The Historic Area is operated by The Colonial Williamsburg Foundation, a nonprofit educational organization staffed

The Reverend Dr. W. A. R. Goodwin with John D. Rockefeller Jr.

by historians, interpreters, actors, administrators, numerous people behind the scenes, and many volunteers.

Williamsburg is a living reminder of our country's past and a guide to its future; it shows us where we have been and can give us clues about where we may be going. Though the stories of the people who lived in the eighteenth-century Williamsburg may seem very different from our lives in the twenty-first century, the heart of the stories remains the same. We created a nation based on new ideas about liberty, independence, and democracy.

Colonial Williamsburg's Historic Area today.

The Colonial Williamsburg: Young Americans books are about individuals who may not have experienced these principles in their own lives, but whose lives foreshadowed changes for the generations that followed. People like the smart and capable Ann McKenzie, who struggled to reconcile her interest in medicine with society's expectations for an eighteenth-century woman. People like the brave Caesar in *Caesar's Story: 1759,* who struggled in silence against the institution of slavery that gripped his people, his family, and himself. While some of these lives evoke painful memories of our country's history, they are a part of that history nonetheless and cannot be forgotten. These stories form the foundation of our country. The people in them are the unspoken heroes of our time.

Childhood in Eighteenth-Century Virginia

If you traveled back in time to Virginia in the 1700s, some things would probably seem familiar to you. Colonial children played some of the same games that children play today: blindman's buff, hopscotch, leapfrog, and hide-and-seek. Girls had dolls, boys flew kites, and both boys and girls might play with puzzles and read.

You might be surprised, however, at how few toys even well-to-do children owned. Adults and children in the 1700s owned far fewer things than we do today, not only fewer toys but also less furniture and clothing. And the books children read were either educational or taught them how to behave properly, ones such as *Aesop's Fables* and the *School of Manners*.

Small children dressed almost alike back then. Boys and girls in prosperous families wore gowns

(dresses) similar to the ones older girls and women wore. Less well-to-do white children and enslaved children wore shifts, which were much like nightgowns. Both black and white boys began wearing pants when they were between five and seven years old.

Boys and girls in colonial Virginia began doing chores when they were six or seven, probably the same age at which *you* started doing chores around the house. But their chores included tasks such as toting kindling, grinding corn with a mortar and pestle, and turning a spit so that meat would roast evenly over the fire.

These chores were done by both black and white children. Many enslaved children also began working

in the fields at this age. They might pick worms off tobacco, carry water to older workers, hoe, or pull weeds. However, they usually were not expected to do as much work as the adults.

As black and white children grew older, they were assigned more and sometimes harder chores. Few children of either race went to school. Those who did usually came from prosperous white families, although there were some charity schools. Some middling (middle-class) and gentry (upper-class) children studied at home with tutors. Other white children learned from their mothers and fathers to read, write, and do simple arithmetic. But not all white children were taught these skills, and very few enslaved children learned them.

When they were ten, eleven, or twelve years old, children began preparing in earnest for adulthood. Boys from well-to-do families got a university education at the College of William and Mary in Williamsburg or at a university in England. Their advanced studies pre-

pared them to manage the plantations they inherited or to become lawyers and important government officials. Many did all three things.

Many middling boys and some poorer ones became apprentices. An apprentice agreed to work for a master for several years, usually until the apprentice turned

twenty-one. The master agreed to teach the apprentice his trade or profession, to ensure that he learned to read and write, and, usually, to feed, clothe, and house him. Apprentices became apothecaries (druggist-doctors), blacksmiths, carpenters, coopers (barrelmakers),

An apprentice with the master cabinetmaker.

founders (men who cast metals in a foundry), merchants, printers, shoemakers, silversmiths, store clerks, and wigmakers. Some girls, usually orphans with no families, also became apprentices. A girl apprentice usually lived with a family and worked as a domestic servant.

Enslaved or free black boys watching tradesmen saw wood.

But most white girls learned at home. Their mothers or other female relatives taught them all the skills they would need to manage their households after they were married —such as cooking, sewing, knitting, cleaning, doing the laundry, managing domestic slaves, and caring for ailing members of the family. Some middling and most gentry girls also learned music, dance, embroidery, and sometimes French. Formal education for girls of all classes, however, was usually limited to reading, writing, and arithmetic.

Enslaved children also began training for adulthood when they were ten to twelve years old. Some boys and girls worked in the house and learned to be domestic slaves. Others worked in the fields. Some boys learned a trade.

Because masters had to pay taxes on slaves who were sixteen or older, slaves were expected to do a full day's work when they turned sixteen, if not sooner. White boys, however, usually were not considered adults until they reached the age of twenty-one. White girls were considered adults when they turned twenty-one or married, whichever came first.

When we look back, we see many elements of colonial childhood that are familiar to us—the love of toys and games, the need to help the family around the house, and the task of preparing for adulthood. However, it is interesting to compare the days of a colonial child to the days of a child today and to see all the ways in which life has changed for children over the years.

Medicine in Eighteenth-Century Virginia

During Ann McKenzie's time, much of the medicine practiced in Virginia was home medicine. Colonial Virginians passed home remedies down from generation to generation, mixing ingredients to soothe ailments such as a cough or sore throat. Those who could read also consulted books such as *Every Man his own Doctor: Or, The Poor Planter's Physician*, which was printed in Williamsburg and Philadelphia in the 1730s.

When home remedies didn't work, and if they could afford it, colonists went to an apothecary, physician, or surgeon. The three were very similar. Most colonial medical practitioners were apothecary-surgeons, like Dr. McKenzie, who dispensed medicines, set broken bones, treated wounds and illnesses, and performed surgery—without anesthesia, which was not invented until the 1800s. Most were addressed as "Doctor," regardless of their training or experience.

Many of the treatments these men used seem strange

A jar of leeches.

to us today. Some pills were made of turpentine and deer dung. A patient might be bled to relieve a fever or stomachache. Leeches could be used to reduce inflammation.

But we should remember that we still do some things that apothecaries, physicians, and surgeons did in the 1700s. The antacids people take for heartburn today contain some of the same ingredients as the chalk lozenges colonial practitioners gave their patients. And doctors today still recommend that people with heartburn avoid eating spicy foods. Some modern doctors even use leeches.

Like today's doctors, eighteenth-century apothecaries, physicians, and surgeons studied to learn their profession. However, most did not attend medical school. (The first medical school in the colonies was established in 1765. Before that, prospective physicians had to travel to Europe for a medical degree.) Instead, they usually worked as apprentices for medical practitioners who agreed to teach them how to make medicines and treat sick people.

Colonial medicine was considered a science, just as modern medicine is today. Apothecaries, physicians, and surgeons did not know then that germs cause disease, but they did observe what made people feel better and what failed to do so. They consulted medical books to learn about old and new treatments. Some experimented with new ways to prevent or cure illnesses, then shared their results with others.

Although colonial practitioners were deeply committed to making their patients well, they did not have the antibiotics or vaccines we have today, so their work was limited to helping people's natural defenses repair injuries or fight illness. Diseases such as smallpox, diphtheria, typhoid, measles, whooping cough, pneumonia, and strep throat were far more dangerous in eighteenth-century Virginia than they are today. The vaccines that prevent some of these diseases were not developed until the nineteenth and twentieth centuries,

Interior of the Pasteur & Galt Apothecary Shop in Colonial Williamsburg's Historic Area.

and the antibiotics that fight bacterial illnesses were not developed until the twentieth century.

Colonists found smallpox especially frightening. The disease spread easily and was deadly. It was not unusual for one out of every four people who contracted it to die. Ports refused to let people off ships on which the illness had broken out until it had run its course, and people avoided going into towns where residents were known to have smallpox.

About 885 people lived in Williamsburg during the smallpox epidemic of 1747 and 1748. At least 747 came down with the illness, and at least 53 died. The epidemic probably affected every person in town. Even the few who did not get sick still had to cope with stores closing, tradespeople being unable to work, farmers refusing to bring produce to market, and sick people needing care. It must have been a terrifying and exhausting time.

Colonists first tried inoculation against smallpox in the 1720s, but, as Dr. McKenzie explained to Ann, many people still didn't trust the procedure in the 1740s. Luckily, safer vaccines have been developed since then. Today we are fortunate that smallpox is no longer a serious threat anywhere in the world. We should remember, though, that there are still diseases that doctors can't prevent or cure. Perhaps 250 years from now, these diseases will pose as little danger to us as smallpox does today.

Colonial Williamsburg Staff

Recipe for Shrewsbury Cakes
(makes 36)

Mrs. McKenzie served Shrewsbury cakes to Mrs. Davenport and Mrs. Blaikley and had Ann take them to Mrs. Geddy as a gesture of friendship. Today we call Shrewsbury cakes sugar cookies. With help from an adult, you can make Shrewsbury cakes using the following recipe.

$1/4$ cup unsalted butter
$1/4$ cup shortening
1 cup sugar (plus extra for rolling the cookies)
$1^1/2$ teaspoons grated orange peel
1 teaspoon vanilla extract
1 egg

146

3 tablespoons milk
2 cups sifted all-purpose flour
1 teaspoon baking soda
$^1/_4$ teaspoon salt
2 teaspoons cream of tartar

Preheat the oven to 350 degrees. Cream together the butter, shortening, and sugar until light and fluffy. Add the orange peel and vanilla extract. Add the egg and milk. Sift together the flour, baking soda, salt, and cream of tartar and add to the creamed mixture. Mix well. Roll the dough into 1-inch balls and roll the balls in sugar. Arrange the balls 1$^1/_2$ inches apart on ungreased cookie sheets. Flatten the balls gently with the bottom of a small glass. Bake in the preheated oven for 8 to 10 minutes or until very light golden brown.

From *Recipes from the Raleigh Tavern Bake Shop,* published by The Colonial Williamsburg Foundation

About the Author

Joan Lowery Nixon was the acclaimed author of more than a hundred books for young readers. She served as president of the Mystery Writers of America and as regional vice president of the Southwest Chapter of that society. She was the only four-time winner of the Edgar Allan Poe Best Juvenile Mystery Award given by the Mystery Writers of America and was also a two-time winner of the Golden Spur Award for best juvenile Western, for two of the novels in her Orphan Train Adventures series.